Sixth Grade
Can Really
Kill You

Sixth Grade Can Really Kill You

Barthe DeClements

AN
APPLE®
PAPERBACK

SCHOLASTIC INC.
New York Toronto London Auckland Sydney

ISBN 0-590-40180-7

Published by Scholastic Inc., 730 Broadway, New York, NY 10003, by arrangement with Viking Penguin, Inc.

12 11 10 9 8 7 6 5 4 3 2   6 7 8 9/8 0 1/9

Printed in the U.S.A.   28

This book is dedicated to the staff and students of Cedar Way Elementary— and especially to Ed Wallace and his sixth-grade class.
I wish to express my thanks to Mark Hammond, Lorna Dunsdon, and Betty Bostrom, Special Education Staff members in the Edmonds School District (Washington), for their professional consultation.

B.D.

Contents

Contents

Sixth Grade Can Really Kill You

Bad Helen

"Oh, Helen," my mother complained, "you're not going to wear those denim pants the first day of school are you?"

"Why not?" I said. "They're clean."

"Let's see if I can find something prettier. How about the yellow skirt Grandma made you?"

"Forget it," I told her, heading for the bathroom. "It's sunny out and I'm not playing baseball in a skirt."

She followed after me, stopping at the doorway to watch me comb my hair. "Curl it a little more by your ears."

I put the comb down.

She took it up. "Here, let me . . ."

"Mother!"

"Well, Liza Minnelli wears her hair brushed forward . . ."

"I'm not Liza Minnelli. I'm Helen."

"But you have those big brown eyes just like her. You should show them off." She moved toward me again, but Dad hollered from the living room, "I'm leaving!" She dropped the comb and hurried downstairs.

I started back to my bedroom, thought a minute, and then turned toward my parents' room. I stood in the middle of the floor, letting my eyes search over the dresser, the bed, *the sewing basket*. That should have something. I opened the basket, picked out one of the smallest spools of thread, and dropped it down the front of my blouse into my bra.

Mother came puffing back up the stairs just as I reached the hall. "What were you doing in there?" she asked sharply.

"Not much."

I could tell she wanted to pat down my clothes by the way her hand fluttered out to me and then up to her chin. "Um . . . Helen, this is a brand-new school year. I just know this is going to be a good one."

"How?" I asked her. "I'm still dumb, you know."

She stayed on my heels as I got my Pee Chee and

my purse off my desk and went down to the front door. When I stretched up to kiss her good-bye, she was busy telling me that she didn't want to hear me say I was *dumb* because I was *not dumb*. Walking down the side walk toward Louise's house, I tried as hard as I could to keep the sickening dread in my stomach from climbing up my throat.

Louise came down her steps with her little sister, Carole, behind her. "I have to haul this thing along to first grade," she told me.

Her little sister shifted her lunch box to her other hand and took my arm. "I'm not bad. And Mom said . . ."

"I know what Mom said. And it doesn't make any difference. Let go of Helen. Only two can walk together, so you walk behind us."

Carole pursed her lips, glared at Louise, and held my arm tighter. Louise gave it up and we started off down the street with Carole yanking on me every time she dodged the bushes at the edge of a yard.

"A bunch of the kids are already there," Louise said as we came in sight of Brier Elementary.

I tried to ignore my stomach.

"I hope I get Mr. Marshall, don't you?"

There was a detour sign hanging on boards in front of the side road. I read it and smiled to myself. DETOUR. D goes toward my right hand. I wiggled the fingers on

5

my right hand to make myself remember. OU is in the middle. . . .

"Don't you hope you get Mr. Marshall?" Louise insisted.

"Sure," I said to Louise. "He's nice." OU, OU, OU, I repeated to myself.

"Listen," she said, "I'll take Carole over to the first grade unit. You wait for me by the sixth-grade unit, O.K.?"

I nodded and she dragged Carole over to the building in front of the office where the little kids were gathered. I went on up the concrete path beside the gym to the building in back of the school. Kids hollered to me as I walked, "Hi, Hel. Hi, Hel." I heard one little girl tell her friend, "That's 'Bad Helen.'"

I waited outside by myself until Stacy joined me. "You cut your hair! It sure is cute," she said.

"My mother's idea." I told her. Stacy has brown hair, too, but hers still hung down her back.

As Louise walked up, she looked both of us over. "You guys are wearing jeans and I'm stuck in this stupid skirt. My mom thinks I have to make a good impression on the teacher the first day."

"Mr. Marshall doesn't care what you wear," Stacy said.

"Did I get him? Did I get him?" Louise asked. "Let's go see."

We crowded into the jammed entrance to the sixth grade rooms and tried to jump up over the other kids' heads to read the class lists that were stuck on the door windows. Louise finally elbowed her way up to Mr. Marshall's door. I watched her leap in the air, and then lean forward again, turn to me, and shake her head.

Just my lousy luck. Well, I wouldn't want him to know anyway.

I was on Mrs. Lobb's list. Whoever that was. When the bell rang, Stacy and Louise filed into Mr. Marshall's room and I went into the room next door with my best I-don't-care smile pasted across my face. Jimmy and Leon were inside and a girl I knew a little bit named Marianne. Jimmy found two empty desks together halfway down the middle aisle and called me to join him. We'd sat next to each other in fourth and fifth grades.

I just barely got settled when Leon came up to Jimmy and gave him a shove. "Get out of the seat, wienie. This is my place."

"Knock it off," Jimmy said. "I was here first."

Leon stuck his knee on the seat and pushed Jimmy over. Jimmy clung to his desk with his hands. "Knock it off, Leon!"

Leon sat down, bumping Jimmy to the floor.

I opened my mouth to object, when a tall woman came into the room, carrying a stack of papers and books. She had gray-black hair and black eyes behind big, black-rimmed glasses. "What are you two boys doing?" she demanded. "Get up off the floor immediately!"

"Leon took my seat," Jimmy explained.

"There are plenty of seats in the back. Take one of those."

Jimmy got up slowly. "Elephant," he mumbled to Leon, who kept smiling straight ahead.

The teacher put her stuff on the big desk in the corner of the room and then went to the blackboard to write MRS. LOBB in large white letters. When she finished, she turned and stared at us. At first some of the kids kept talking. She kept on staring until the noise in the room dribbled down to silence.

"I'm Mrs. Lobb," she said. "We're going to be together a whole year and I expect to enjoy you and I hope you enjoy having me."

The way the kids' glances slid toward each other, I doubted that.

"Now I think the first thing we'll do this morning is have an arithmetic review. Who would like to pass out the books?"

Ten hands were raised and kids squealed, "Me, me, me!"

Mrs. Lobb stared stonily at the room until the squealing stopped and hands wilted down. "This is the sixth grade. Not the dog pound." She pointed to Sharon

Hinkler. "You raised your hand quietly. You may pass out the books."

Sharon got up, trying to hide her smile, went to the front table, and started counting out books. She took five at a time to each row and then went back for more. Two monitors could have done it faster, but nobody said anything.

Mrs. Lobb wrote PAGE 11 on the board. When I got my book, I turned quickly to page 11. A review of fractions. That would be easy. After everyone received a book, and we had written our names inside and written the book numbers on the sheet Mrs. Lobb passed around, she told us to take out paper and pencils and do the first six problems.

Jack Hanson was in the seat behind me. I didn't know him very well because he hadn't been in Miss Jewell's room in fifth grade. Anyway, as soon as I got out my Pee Chee, he poked me in the back and whispered to lend him some paper. I took out an extra sheet and held it over my shoulder. After I felt Jack take it, I concentrated on dividing fractions. I was the first one done.

When most of the kids were finished, Mrs. Lobb asked who would like to put the first problem on the board. "I would!" Jimmy said and got the steely stare.

"What about you?" She nodded to me. "It didn't seem to take you very long."

I went up to the board with my paper and wrote $24\frac{1}{2} \div 5\frac{1}{4} = \frac{49}{2} \div \frac{21}{4} = \frac{49}{2} \times \frac{4}{21}$. I crossed out the two, changed the four to a two, and multiplied. My first answer was $\frac{98}{21}$. I divided each number by seven and wrote my final answer, which was $4\frac{2}{3}$.

"Very good." Mrs. Lobb smiled at me. "You must be a smart girl."

"Hah!" Leon said, as I hurried to my seat.

At lunch recess, I waited for Louise and Stacy outside Mr. Marshall's room. Diane Gates, Jenny Sawyer, and Elsie Edwards followed them out. Diane had the bat and ball. "Come on, Hel," she said to me. "Let's get a game going."

We all trooped out to the field together. Sharon Hinkler, who'd been waiting outside Mr. Marshall's room, too, ran alongside Diane trying to tell her about Mrs. Lobb. Diane ignored her so Sharon dropped back to walk quietly beside Jenny and Elsie.

The boys already had the sixth-grade diamond, but they agreed to play boys against girls. Jack pitched for their side and I pitched for ours.

Diane and Stacy are our best hitters. Jenny and Louise are O.K. Elsie isn't quite as good as Jenny. Elsie used to be really fat last year, but she's lost a lot of weight and can run fast. Sharon spends most of her time at bat complaining about the pitches.

We got in only two innings before the bell rang. The

boys beat us 3 to 2. Mostly because of Jimmy's home run. During the game I was having such a good time, I forgot about school. Going back in, though, my stomach started to hurt. We hadn't had reading in the morning so we were certain to get it in the afternoon.

Sure enough, Mrs. Lobb had written on the blackboard: Reading–1:10, Art–2:00, Music–2:40. Before we began our work, she announced that she had a treat for us. She pulled her roll-around chair to the front of the room and settled down to read aloud from *Old Yeller*. I could hardly pay attention to the story because prickles kept running up and down my arms. At two minutes after one, I couldn't sit still any longer.

Keeping my eyes on everyone around me, I slipped the spool of thread out of my bra. I slowly leaned forward and tied the end of the thread on the leg of my desk, and, keeping my eye on Mrs. Lobb, I laced the spool around Leon's desk and back to my desk and back to Leon's desk.

Leon frowned down at me and whispered, "What are you, a spider?"

Mrs. Lobb looked up. Leon sat up straight. I sat up straight. She returned to *Old Yeller* and I finished the barricade.

Marianne was chosen to pass out the reading books. I barely paid attention when a book was put on my desk. I was busy lettering my sign, which read: *betour*.

I was sure I had it correct because I remembered that *d* goes toward my right hand and *ou* is in the middle.

I took a piece of Scotch tape out of my desk. As I stuck the sign on the back of my chair, I grinned at Jack. He looked at the paper, perplexed. I pointed to the web between Leon and me before turning around.

"What's a bee-tour?" Jack's voice hissed in my ear.

I was going to lean back and tell him, "That's a D, stupid," when I froze. What if I was wrong? I couldn't be wrong. I knew I remembered.

My eyes focused on the alphabet above the blackboard. Capital *D* went to the right. *Little d went to the left*. I snatched my sign away, crumpled it in my hand, and slid down in my seat, my face hot with embarrassment.

The Blob

Mrs. Lobb's assignment was to read the first story in the book and answer the questions at the end. The story was about a boy and his dying grandfather. I tried to read it without following along with my finger, but I kept getting mixed up. At two o'clock, I was only on page 3, while most of the kids were working on the questions. Mrs. Lobb said we'd have time to finish the next day and to put away our books.

For art we did something called "the natural way to draw." We were supposed to draw a fern Mrs. Lobb had placed on a stool. Only we were to draw without looking at our papers. Sort of feel the sides of it with our eyes, Mrs. Lobb said.

I was squinting at one of the frilly leaves, when Mrs. Lobb walked up the aisle. "Very good," she said to me.

Out of the corner of my eye, I saw her tip Leon's head up from his paper before she moved on. Then there was a loud "Awp!" and Mrs. Lobb's arms began flapping as she fought to keep from sprawling over Roy, who sat in front of Leon.

Oh, oh, the barricade!

Roy jumped out of his seat as Mrs. Lobb landed across his desk. Leon had his hand over his mouth, trying not to laugh. Jack wasn't even trying.

Mrs. Lobb shakily pushed herself upright, took a big breath, and peered down at my web. "What in the world's all this thread doing here?"

I heard a mumble from the back of the room, "Bad Helen strikes again." Jimmy, no doubt.

"Who put this here?" Mrs. Lobb demanded.

Leon fended her off with both hands. "Not me. Not me."

She turned to Roy.

"No way," Roy said.

She looked at me.

I stared back at her with my head scrunched into my shoulders.

"Did you do this?" She had both hands on her hips now. "Well, answer me. Did you?"

I nodded.

"Is this the way you usually start out the school year?"

"You bet." Jimmy's voice drifted from the back of the room.

But this time she heard him. "What did you say, young man?"

"Uh, nothing," Jimmy answered.

She focused back on me. "I think the best thing for you to do, miss, is to go out in the hall and write an apology to me and your classmates."

I rose from my seat.

"Take your pencil and paper with you."

I did.

Sitting on the hall floor, I carefully wrote out the apology:

> I didnt mene to mak you fall.
> Helen Nichols

There was a burst of laughter from our room. I got up and peeked through the door window. Mrs. Lobb was arranging Leon on the stool for a class model. I could see Jack at his desk rolling little balls of paper in his fingers. Somebody was going to get it in the back of the neck. When Mrs. Lobb moved away from Leon, I ducked out of sight.

It got massively boring in the hall. I went into the girls' lavatory, came out, paced up and down, and finally decided I might as well decorate the wall. Just as I started on a capital F, Jack came out the classroom door. I felt weird around him, after my goof with the sign, so I kept my eyes on my work.

"What are you doing?" he asked.

"Nothing," I said. "What are you doing out here?"

"The Blob sent me out."

I laughed and then went back to my printing. The paint was so slick I had trouble making the pencil line show.

Jack came up behind me. "Hey, let's knock that off."

"What?" I turned to face him. I might be the rowdiest girl in the school, but Jack is one of the rowdiest boys.

"Erase that."

"No!"

He snatched my pencil out of my hand and scrubbed the eraser across the wall.

"Where do you get off?" I asked him.

"Listen," he said, "they'll remember who was out in the hall and *I'll* be the one to get the swats, not you."

I felt a large figure move up the outside walk. "Here comes the principal," I said.

Jack glanced quickly out the window, handed me my pencil, and disappeared into the boys' john.

The letters were almost gone, but I backed up against them anyway as Mr. Douglas swung the door open.

When he saw me, he raised his eyebrows. "Couldn't you have made it through the first day, Helen?"

"I guess not."

"When you have a nice new teacher?"

"What's nice about her?"

"Now, Helen . . ."

"I just wondered."

He looked down at me with a stern expression on his face. "Just remember, we don't pass sixth-graders unless we're sure they're ready for junior high. You'd better do a little thinking about how you're going to show us you're ready."

There was no use telling him that I didn't care about junior high. I just wanted to get out of school, period. Before I could think of a decent answer, Miss Sleek, the music teacher, popped through the outside door. I like her. She dresses like a rocker and is a smart-mouth, too.

"Oh, my favorite little soprano and my big principal." She tapped Mr. Douglas on the shoulder. "Are you going to sing with us today?"

"I . . . ah . . . no. I was just seeing how things are going on out here." He hurried through Mr. Marshall's door. Miss Sleek ruffled my hair before she went into the music room.

Jack eased out of the boys' john. "Is he gone?"

"No," I told him. "He went in to see Mr. Marshall."

"I'm going to get killed if I take a discipline slip home this afternoon."

"Maybe Mrs. Lobb doesn't know about those yet."

"Fat chance," he said.

He was probably right. All the teachers knew about the discipline slips, even on the first day. Our class began to file out of our room. Jack moved over to lean against the wall with me.

When the last kid had gone into music, Mrs. Lobb came to the door and told us to come in. We followed her over to her desk. "Have you got your apology?" she asked me.

I handed it to her.

Without looking up from my paper, she asked, "How do you spell 'mean'?"

I didn't answer.

"*M-e-a-n,*" Jack said.

She regarded him coldly. "Do you think I meant you?"

Jack shrugged. "I don't know."

She put the paper on her desk. "I think we need to come to an understanding right now. I believe my job here is to teach students. I think your job is to learn. Is that right?"

We both nodded.

"Now if you're going to waste my time, your time,

18

and the other students' time playing, we're not going to get along very well. I'll overlook what happened today because you may not have thought of a school as a place where you get down to business as soon as you enter. But that's how it's going to be in my room. And by the looks of your paper, young lady, I would say you had a lot of work to do."

I took in a slow breath. Jack didn't move a muscle.

She waved her hand, dismissing us. "Now go on in the music room and behave yourselves."

That was no problem. Nobody's bad in Miss Sleek's class.

After school, I waited for Louise and we walked over to the first-grade room to pick up her little sister. She came bouncing out with two stickers on her forehead. "Look at me! Look at me!" Carole demanded.

"We can see you," Louise told her. "How'd you get them?"

"One for being quiet in the line and one for raising my hand before I talked. Isn't that good?"

"Tremendous," Louise said. She turned to me as we crossed the street toward home. "Somebody said you were out in the hall with Jack Hanson."

"True," I agreed.

"What'd he say?"

"I don't know. The usual."

"I think redheads are so cute, don't you?"

"Why redheads?" Carole asked.

"I wasn't talking to you," Louise snapped.

I stopped cold on the sidewalk. "I forgot my reading book."

"Big deal," Louise said. "It won't matter the first day."

"Yes, it will. I'll catch ya later." I ran all the way back to school. Mrs. Lobb wasn't at her desk, but the room was open so I dashed in and got my book.

When I reached home, Mother opened the door with a smile. "Well, I bet your school day didn't turn out as bad as you thought it would."

"Worse," I said.

Double Saved

After I shed my jacket, I put a bunch of grapes and crackers on a plate and Mother and I sat down at the dining room table to work on my reading assignment. She kept telling me to please try reading without pointing my finger. I kept telling her that if I didn't use my finger I would lose my place.

"Well, just practice it a little," she said.

So I practiced it a little and couldn't keep track of the sentences.

"Keep practicing," she said. "You're in the sixth grade now."

"I know. I know," I told her through clenched teeth.

"Getting upset will just make it harder, Helen. Go on reading while I put the macaroni on."

I kept reading while she put the macaroni on and while she grated the cheese beside me, correcting every third word. I was still reading when Dad got home.

"Ah, back to the old routine," he said, giving us each a kiss.

"Unfortunately," I added.

"Well," he patted me on the head, "only seven more years to go."

"Four more years. Washington state law says you can quit school when you complete the ninth grade or are sixteen years old."

Mother got up from the table. "Helen, we're not even going to consider that."

Maybe *you're* not, I thought to myself.

After dinner I put the dishes in the dishwasher, took my reading book back out, and started to work on the questions. It was ten o'clock before I wrote my final copy with all Mother's spelling corrections.

On the way to school in the morning, Louise rattled away about how neat it was that Mr. Marshall taught sixth grade this year instead of P.E., like he had last year. I didn't think it was so neat. I liked the way he coached sports. P.E. and singing and math were the only things I was good in. I needed those three As to make up for the Ds I got in reading, spelling, and social studies.

It must have sunk into Louise that my class wasn't as great as hers, because suddenly she said, "I wonder what Mrs. Lobb will do for P.E. Maybe she'll be one of those teachers who just lets you play games for the whole period. Those kind are all right as long as they don't referee."

Mrs. Lobb did let us play a game for P.E. She said we might as well take advantage of the good weather while we had it. The refereeing gave her a problem, though. Before we left for the field, she asked the class to name the student who knew the most about baseball.

"Jack! Jack! Helen! Jack! Helen!" the kids shouted.

Mrs. Lobb lowered her eyelids while she let out a long sigh. The shouting stopped and hands went up. Mrs. Lobb called on Sharon.

Sharon pursed her lips, thinking a minute before she answered. "I guess Jack does. Or Helen."

Mrs. Lobb chose Jack to be the referee—although, I don't think she wanted either one of us. She said Marianne could be captain for one side, and Leon could be captain for the other.

Out on the field, Jack flipped a nickel to see which captain got first picks. It was Leon and he picked me. Marianne picked Roy. Leon picked Jimmy. At the very end of the pickings came Sharon, Dawn, and a near-sighted boy named Ernest.

Leon put me on first base, which made Jimmy moan. "Come on, Leon, let her pitch."

"I'm going to pitch," Leon told him.

Jack interrupted the argument by saying, "Batter up."

Leon took his place on the mound and threw his first ball.

"Ball one!" Jack called.

"Come on, Leon, trade places with Helen," Jimmy pleaded from second base.

"Back off, wienie!" Leon snarled before pitching ball two.

"Elephant!" Jimmy yelled.

Leon whirled around. "I said, 'Back off, wienie!' "

Mrs. Lobb marched out to the mound. "Give me the ball."

Leon handed it to her.

"Now you students can make up your mind to either play the game without arguing and calling each other names or we'll return to the classroom."

Total silence.

"Well?" she asked.

"We'll be nice," Jimmy assured her.

"Ya, we'll be good," Leon said.

"All right, see that you are. And that goes for

everyone." She gave Leon back the ball.

The rest of the inning was without hassles even though there were four walks. Jimmy kept his eyes focused on the ground when he came in from the field. Before we went out for the second inning, Leon tossed me the ball. "Here, you pitch this one."

I got Dawn out on three strikes. Sharon was up next. She blinked as the ball went by her.

"Strrrike one!" Jack called.

I pitched to the lower left corner.

"Strrrike two!"

Sharon dropped the bat and put her hands on her hips. "That was way low, Jack."

Jack shook his head. "Strike two."

She looked appealingly at Mrs. Lobb, who made no comment. Sighing, Sharon picked up the bat. I sent the third pitch right across the plate. She slashed away, three inches under the ball.

Jack threw his arm in the air. "Strike three and you're out."

Sharon stomped off to complain to Marianne about my pitching.

Roy came up to bat. I leaned forward to eye the catcher. She cupped her glove low. I leaned back for the pitch.

"Burn it over the plate, Hel!" Jimmy hollered.

Mrs. Lobb waved her arms. "That will be all."

"What's going on?" Jack asked. "It isn't time to go in."

"I gave you all fair warning. Line up, please. Ernie, get the base bags."

As the kids from the outfield walked in slowly, Jack, Leon, and Jimmy circled in front of Mrs. Lobb. "What'd we do wrong?" Jimmy asked.

"You know very well what you did," Mrs. Lobb told him. "You called Helen a name."

"But that isn't a bad name," Jack objected. "That's a nickname. Like you just called Ernest 'Ernie.' "

"Ya, and all the teachers call Stacia 'Stacy.' So we call Helen—ah—by—by the first of her name," Leon tried to explain.

Mrs. Lobb gave him a stern look. "Not in my class you don't. That isn't a nice way to refer to a girl. Now get in line. We're going in."

So we gathered up the ball and bats, filed back to the classroom, and did our social studies in resentful silence. I hate social studies because it's just like reading, only harder. It was a relief when I heard the lunch cart in the hall.

While I swallowed down the rubbery school Jell-O, I watched Mrs. Lobb put our afternoon schedule on the blackboard. Reading, spelling, and science. Would she have oral reading today? I hadn't had any time to practice the next story in the book. If she called on me, I was doomed. I pushed the rest of my lunch away and slunk down in my seat.

Leon looked over at me. "Aren't you going to eat your chocolate cake?" I passed him my tray.

After noon recess, my sweating really started. I sat up straight, clenched my fingers together. I sat back in my seat, running my hands down my legs. Nothing I did helped the waiting. It seemed like Mrs. Lobb would never put down *Old Yeller*.

Finally she rose from her chair and told us to take out our reading books and turn to page 17. It was a play. If I could avoid getting a part, I'd be O.K. Or if I got a little part, maybe I could skip ahead and check out the words.

With my finger I followed down the list of characters as Mrs. Lobb divided out the important ones among the waving hands. At the end of the list there were small parts with the names, Clerk, Customer in Toy Store, and Little Child.

I got Clerk. I flipped through the play fast to see how many lines I had. Only about seven. Saved! And we didn't even have to do the play right away. Mrs. Lobb said we could finish up yesterday's reading questions and then practice our parts silently. Double saved.

Doomsday

The next morning I got ready for school without hating
the day. It was raining and I still didn't hate it. Mother
kept looking out the window as Dad and I ate breakfast.
"I knew all that sunshine was too good to last. I suppose
our summer's over now and it will rain for the next nine
months. I was hoping my pumpkins would be able to
ripen this year."

My mother's big on gardening. Most of our backyard's in vegetables and raspberries. Louise's yard is
full of cages for her French Lops. She started out with
two rabbits, but, as she says, they got out of hand.

Mother walked to the door with Dad. Then, when I
was ready, she walked to the door with me. "This will

be a good day for you," she said. "You've got your social studies and spelling done and your part in the play is letter-perfect."

I smiled back at her when she kissed me. What was neat about the day was if I read my part smoothly, then, later, if we had to read aloud and I hadn't had time to practice, it might sound like I got mixed up by mistake. I could sort of laugh and go over the paragraph again like kids do when they goof up.

Louise came out of her house boiling mad and almost slammed the door on Carole. She stamped down the steps to where I was standing on the sidewalk. "Look at this rain jacket she made me wear! It's two inches short in the sleeves!"

She stretched out her arms, dangling her lunch bag in one hand. The jacket *was* too small for her. There are five kids in the Martin family, so each one has to take a turn at getting new clothes.

"And besides," she raged as we walked along the wet sidewalk, "I can't have a birthday party."

"That's because Mama has to pay all that money for rabbit feed because you didn't earn the money like you said you would." Carole dodged away from a dripping rhododendron, making me stumble over her.

"Walk in back like I told you to," Louise ordered her sister. "Stop hanging on Helen. You know the way now. You don't need to come with us."

When Carole didn't let go of my arm, Louise reached across me and yanked her loose. "Now walk in back and I mean it!"

Carole walked in back, running up to us every now and then to step on Louise's heels until Louise turned around and swatted her.

When we got to school, we saw a tall, skinny boy and a lady go into the office.

"He looks like a sixth-grader," Louise said. "Not too cute, though."

Mr. Douglas brought the boy to our room as Mrs. Lobb was marking absences down in her roll book. She introduced him to us and put him in the empty seat in front of me. His name was Warren Keller. He smelled like he hadn't changed his socks for a week.

Since I had all my assignments done, the day went pretty easy. I wasn't even worried when we got to reading. I turned to page 17 and sat back to listen to the kids start the play.

Mrs. Lobb stood in front of us with her book open. "Let's see now. What will we give Warren to do? Perhaps you better do Sharon's part, Helen, since she's absent. Warren can be the Clerk."

I put up my hand.

When Mrs. Lobb nodded, I said in a rush, "Why doesn't Warren just take Sharon's part? I don't know it any better than he does."

"Sharon was the Daughter, dummy," Leon whispered.

Mrs. Lobb raised her eyebrows at Leon. "I think Warren might be more comfortable playing the part of the Clerk," she said to me. "Now, let's get started. Marianne, you're the narrator."

"*The Doll in the Lace Dress,*" Marianne announced the title. As she read the description of the opening scene in the shopping mall, I frantically searched through the play for the Daughter's lines. They were on every page. I was dead.

"Helen, you're first," Mrs. Lobb prompted.

I turned back to the beginning of the play. " 'Daughter: Oh, look . . .' "

"Don't read the character's name, Helen. Just read what she says."

"O.K." I took a breath. " 'Oh, look at that na— na—na . . .' "

Someone giggled.

Jack poked me in the back. "Nativity."

" 'Oh, look at that nativity skene.' "

More giggles.

"Scene, scene," Jack whispered.

" 'Nativity scene.' " My cheeks burned and I knew my face was flaming red.

" 'The Mother and Daughter walk along until they come to a toy store window,' " Marianne read.

31

Dawn's turn. " 'What an exquisite collection of dolls.' "

My turn. " 'Isn't the one in the lace dress pu—pa—paint.' "

"Quaint, quaint," Jack said.

"Excuse me, 'quaint.' " I caught Mrs. Lobb's puzzled stare. I was dead, dead, dead.

Dawn's turn. " 'Wouldn't Melinda love getting that doll Christmas morning?' "

" 'Yes, but I'm sure it is too . . .' "

"Expensive," Jack put in quickly.

" 'Expensive.' " I finished.

It went on like that. Forever. Mrs. Lobb made the kids quit giggling, but it was still more horrible than my worst nightmare. When the play was finally over, I put my book in my desk and kept my head down while I secretly tried to pull my sticky blouse away from my sweaty skin.

Mrs. Lobb passed out a ditto sheet of health questions. She said we were to turn in our answers before we went to music. I propped my forehead up with my hand while I worked so nobody could see my face. When Mrs. Lobb collected the papers she looked quickly over mine. I knew what my mother was going to get.

Mrs. Lobb told us to line up for music. I took a place next to the blackboard and concentrated on the chalk tray. Jack came right up beside me. "You sure read terrible."

"I know."

"No talking, please," Mrs. Lobb said. "Now go quietly into the music room."

I watched the floor while we marched into the hall, but Jack bumped me to make me look at him. "You sure pitch good, though."

"Big deal," I said.

Miss Sleek had a record for us to listen to before we started a new song. I couldn't even hear it. I didn't even try to sing. When we lined up to go back to our room, she came up from behind me, put her arms around me, and whispered in my ear, "You look like you could use a big hug."

I heard Mother talking on the phone as I opened the front door. Just what I figured. She was saying, "Helen's already been given a reading and IQ test at the University of Washington. She has normal intelligence. In fact, she's quite bright. . . . We are perfectly aware that she has a reading problem. . . . No, we are not going to consider special education. . . . I'm sorry, but if we don't sign permission, it won't do you any good to recommend it. . . . Well, that may be how it was in your former school district, but here a child cannot be transferred to a special class without parents' permission. We are working with her at home and . . ."

I went upstairs. I didn't need to hear the rest. Mother came into my room about twenty minutes later. "How come you're lying down?" she asked. "Don't you feel well?"

"I feel terrible."

She sat on the edge of my bed. "Now, Helen, there's no use getting upset."

"What if I don't pass sixth grade?"

"You'll pass," she assured me. "You always pass."

"I flunked a science paper today."

"That's just one paper. Your teachers have always averaged everything in and your homework will get you through." She took my hand. "Come on. Let's get at it."

I pulled my hand away. "I don't have any homework."

"Of course you do."

"No, I don't! Mother, go on downstairs and get dinner or something." I flopped over, burying my face in my pillow.

She left, but was back again in fifteen minutes. "Louise is on the phone."

"Oh, for . . ." I got up.

Louise was all breathless and happy. "Guess what, Helen? My brother Christian says he'll take us to the carnival in Lynnwood for my birthday Friday. And Mom says I can have you over for my birthday dinner and you get to stay all night. Isn't that great? You can, can't you?"

"I suppose so. I'll ask."

"Beg real hard and tell me tomorrow morning, O.K.?"

When I hung up, Mother wanted to know what that was all about. "Louise's birthday is Friday," I told her, "and I'll have to get her a present."

I wandered out into the backyard. It had stopped raining. The sun coming out from behind the clouds sent steam up from the tops of the corn tassels. I sifted the yellow silk between my fingers.

How would I know scene doesn't sound like skene? How come everyone knows when *c* sounds like *s* except me? I don't get that—*p* faces the left and *q* faces the right. Or *q* faces the left? I wanted to throw up.

Heads Up

Mother opened my bedroom door. "Helen, come on down and eat now while it's hot. You can dress after breakfast."

"I don't want anything to eat," I told her.

"You have to eat. Now get up. Nothing's worse than cold eggs."

"There are a lot of things worse than cold eggs." But she didn't hear me. She'd already gone downstairs. I pulled myself out of bed.

Mother plopped a plate under my nose as soon as I was seated. I turned my head away. Eggs smell awful when you don't feel good.

"Off your feed?" Dad asked.

"You could say that."

Mother brought her coffee cup to the table. She eyed my untouched food. Before an argument started, I brought up Louise's birthday.

"We can drive down to Aurora Village and get her a present this afternoon," Mother said.

"And she asked me to dinner and to stay all night."

"I don't know about all night. You have your studies to do this weekend."

"Let the poor kid have some time off," Dad said. "You're going to have her hating school more than she does now."

"If that's possible," I added.

"Oh, Helen . . ." Mother began.

I pushed back my chair. "Well, do I get to go or not? I'm supposed to tell Louise this morning."

"Yes, and have a good time," Dad said. "We'll go out to dinner with the Lindstroms."

Mother's eyes widened in alarm. "I don't—I don't know what I'd wear."

"Buy something," he told her.

I went upstairs to dress. Before I left the house I checked the bathroom cabinet, found a sample tube of toothpaste, and shoved it into the pocket of my jeans.

At school I stayed out in the hall talking to Louise about her birthday until the bell rang. I didn't really expect the kids in my room to say anything to me about the play. Most kids just tell each other, "Helen's dumb," and go on with their work.

Our room challenged Marshall's to a baseball game during noon recess. Diane didn't think that was too fair because Jack, Jimmy, and I were all on one team. It started to rain halfway through the second inning. Then hail pelted down and bounced in the grass.

Jimmy dropped the ball and tipped his head back, trying to catch the hail in his mouth. Jack and Leon tried it, too. The hail stung my face. Anyway, it was a good chance for me to disappear.

I kept an eye on the playground aide while I slipped around the gym. We aren't supposed to go back to our units during recess. Not to use the lavatory or anything. When I got to the walkway, I hurried along in a businesslike manner, as if I were on an errand for a teacher or something.

Mrs. Lobb wasn't in the room. I fished the toothpaste out of my pocket with one hand while I pulled her chair out with the other. I squirted the toothpaste along the front edge of the seat—high enough up so it wouldn't slop down on the floor and low enough so she probably wouldn't see it. I pushed the chair back to the desk, screwed the top on the toothpaste, dropped it in the hall garbage can, and got out of there.

When we were all quietly seated, Mrs. Lobb took

Old Yeller off her desk and steered her chair to the center of the room.

"Hey, there's something on . . ."

I gave Warren a fast punch in the back.

Mrs. Lobb looked up. Warren didn't volunteer anything more. *Old Yeller* is a pretty interesting story when you have a chance to listen to it. Little Arliss is my favorite character.

Mrs. Lobb finished the chapter, closed the book, and stood up to wheel her chair back.

"A birdie doo-dooed on Mrs. Blob," Leon whispered.

I put a hand over my mouth to cover my giggles. Mrs. Lobb frowned at the faint sound of conversation and told us to take out our reading books and turn to page 36. We did.

Once we were quietly working, Sharon went up to the teacher's desk. "I think you've got some of your lunch on your clothes," Sharon said.

Mrs. Lobb looked down at her black suit. "Where?"

"It's in the back."

Mrs. Lobb rose from her chair, twisted around, and peered over her big bottom. "Oh, my goodness! How did that happen?"

She got a Kleenex off her desk and tried to scrub the toothpaste away. She used four tissues before she gave it up. "I'll have to wash this off," she said.

"Sharon, you be monitor until I get back."

Sharon stood importantly in front of the room watching us work.

"Hey, Hel, heads up!" Jimmy called from the back blackboard.

Jack ducked as I barely caught the eraser whizzing toward me. Leon scrambled to the side wall in time for me to zip it to him. Jack yelled, "Here, here!" from behind the bookcase.

The principal opened the door. I melted into my seat as the boys eased toward theirs.

"What's going on in here?" Mr. Douglas demanded. "Where's your teacher?"

"She's in the lavatory," Sharon said in a small voice.

He nodded toward her. "Go sit down. Every one of you, put your heads down."

After a few minutes, I heard the classroom door open and Mrs. Lobb exclaim, "Oh, Mr. Douglas."

He asked her to step out in the hall. The door didn't latch behind them and we heard his rumbling voice and her protesting squeaks.

"Boy, is she getting it," Leon said.

"I heard my mother say," Sharon informed us, "that teachers aren't supposed to leave their classes unattended."

By Friday the story had reached my mother via the phone line. She stood at my bedroom door watching

40

me put pajamas into my overnight bag. "Mrs. Hinkler called and said your teacher left your class alone yesterday."

"So?"

"Well, does she do that often?"

"No." I opened my dresser drawer to get out clean socks and underpants.

She ran her hand over her newly frosted hair. "I dread going out with the Lindstroms tonight."

"Why? I thought they were Dad's clients."

"They are, but Anna Lindstrom always looks so perfect and I always overdo it or underdo it. I don't see why they're interested in going out with their C.P.A."

"Maybe they like Dad." I gathered up my bag and jacket. "Let me out, O.K. I have to get my toothbrush."

She followed me into the bathroom, still talking nervously about the dinner with the Lindstroms. "I felt like an idiot the time they invited us to sit in their box at the horse races. When we got to Longacres, I found Anna and her friends in jeans and tennis shoes and I was wearing a pink pants suit."

"Well, I gotta go," I kissed her good-bye. "I'll see ya tomorrow."

"Make it before noon," she called after me.

Louise met me at her door, took the album present I was carrying, and had the birthday wrapping torn off before we even reached the living room. "Aw right,

Van Halen. I love David Lee Roth, don't you?"

I sat down on the davenport beside her. "I like Eddie Van Halen best."

"His grin's dynamite. But the hair on David Lee Roth's chest! Couldn't you just imagine running your fingers over it?"

I couldn't. Louise and I are different. We don't even look the same. She's sort of round all over with medium blond hair, white skin, and blue eyes. I've got dark brown hair, olive skin, and I've got busts, but not as much as Louise.

Sometimes I wonder why we're friends because we're so different. Her house even smells different than mine. My mother tries to keep fresh flowers in a bowl, especially roses or honeysuckle. Sometimes when I come to breakfast in the morning, the sweet scent of honeysuckle has drifted through the whole downstairs.

Louise's mother is Italian. She says I look more like her kid than Louise does. Mrs. Martin is plumper than her daughters. She usually has a white apron on with flour smudges and streaks of tomato sauce across the middle. Her kitchen smells of olive oil and garlic. A good smell, though.

She piles your plate up with spaghetti and vegetables. I like it all except the Italian olives. They're too greasy for me. Mr. Martin is German. He repaired clocks in Germany, but here he repairs jewelry.

He came home just as Louise was putting the record on the family stereo. "Ah, what is this?" he asked. "Purple ribbons and paper with violets on it. A birthday?"

Louise came over to hug him. "Come on, Dad, I know you didn't forget. Where have you got it?"

As she searched through his pockets, he threw back his head. "What is this? What is this? My own daughter?"

Mrs. Martin stood in the kitchen doorway smiling. Carole scooted around her, followed by the oldest sister, Margaret. They watched Louise fend off her father's hands to reach the inside pocket of his jacket.

Louise pulled out a small domed box and pried it open. "Oh, wow, an aquamarine! I love it, I love it!"

"Lemme see. Lemme see." Carole stood on tiptoe while Louise slipped the ring on her finger.

Louise passed her hand under everyone's nose. "See, see." She ended up back near her father and threw her arms around him. "You always know just what I love."

After we ate, Louise and I went out to the backyard to play with her rabbits until Christian came home. Christian is eighteen and he works at Pantley's in Lynnwood during the dinner hour. Louise says he makes lots of money in tips. He has a fiberglass car he built called a Futura. It looks like a Corvette and you sit in it with your feet straight out. My dad predicts that it will crumble up like cardboard if Christian ever has a wreck, so

I never tell my mother when Louise and I get to ride in it.

We had just put Red Eyes back in his cage when Christian came out. "You aren't even ready," he said to Louise.

"Yes, we are," she told him.

"You aren't going in that tank top."

Louise strutted in front of him. "This is risqué."

"You mean risky," Christian said. "Go change."

"No!"

"O.K., I guess I'll save on gas."

"Oh, all right!" Louise headed toward the house. "Brothers!"

Christian let us off in front of the Fred Meyer shopping center and said he'd meet us in exactly the same spot in two hours.

"Only two hours?" Louise complained. Christian gave her a look and she said quickly, "O.K., O.K. We'll be here."

"And happy birthday." He leaned across the seat holding a bill in his hand.

Louise snatched it up. "Five dollars! Thank you, thank you, brother dear."

As soon as Christian pulled out, Louise headed for the parking lot. "We can get a wad of tickets with this. I hope Leon's here tonight, don't you?"

"Not especially," I said.

We rode on the Scrambler first and then the Hurricane. On the way over to the Hammerhead, we bumped into Jimmy. I was glad to have him join us, but Louise ignored him. She wanted to find Leon.

She spotted him coming down on the Hammerhead and made her way through the crowd, urging Jimmy and me to hurry up. Leon didn't look too good. The attendant lifted up the bar crossing the seat and Leon got out shakily.

"How about going up again?" Louise asked him.

He brushed past her. She watched him leave, shrugged her shoulders, and said to us, "We might as well climb in."

She had one foot in the cage when she backed up. "Oh, ick!"

The attendant came up behind her with a pail of water to wash Leon's puke away.

Shoot the Duck

My birthday had been in the summer when we were visiting Grandma, so I hadn't had a party, either. Mother said I could have one in the fall. I decided on a skating party and invited Stacy, Diane, Jenny, Elsie, and Marianne. And Louise, of course. Louise wanted me to invite boys, but I didn't because boys always wreck the place. We had tacos and sundaes at my house, and then Dad drove us all to the rink.

As soon as we turned in our shoes at the counter, we heard the announcer say, "O.K., you lovebirds, it's couple time. All you gals get out there and grab the guys."

Stacy, Louise, and Diane snatched up their skates and dived for the benches. While tightening their laces, they peeked through their eyelashes at the boys lounging against the snack bar. "That blond in the blue half-shirt is cute," Louise said.

"You're right." Diane slipped off the bench, skated over to the snack bar, and picked off the blond, leaving seconds for Stacy and Louise.

Elsie, Jenny, Marianne, and I watched our friends circling the rink. Each time we saw Louise pass by, she was giggling into her partner's face. "She's going to go on her butt," Elsie predicted.

Sure enough, when the announcer called out, "O.K., everybody turn around—it's reverse skating," Louise stumbled, tripped her partner, and fell on top of him.

"Short romance," Jenny said, as we watched the boy limp to the sidelines.

"Clear the rink," the announcer ordered. "Everybody get ready for Red Light, Green Light."

Our whole group was up for that one. We plastered ourselves against the end wall with the rest of the racing crowd. Three judges waited in front of us.

"Green light," a judge called out, and we were off.

"Red light!" a judge yelled and whirled to catch any moving skater.

"Green light!" We were off again.

"Red light!" A judge caught Diane skidding to a stop and sent her back to the starting line.

"Green light!" The judges zoomed around the floor with the skaters hot behind them.

"Red light!" Half the crowd was back to start.

"Green light!" "Red light!" "Green light!" "Red light!" "Green light!"

I hit the finish line first and got a little slip of paper that said FREE PEPSI. The place was hot and stunk with sweat by that time and I gulped down the whole cup.

"O.K.," the announcer said, "everybody ready for Shoot the Duck. Get out on the floor if you want to compete."

"I'll go for it," Elsie said.

"Me, too," Marianne said.

The music started and we three moved warily around the rink with the other skaters.

"Shoot the duck!" the announcer said.

We knelt, sliding forward on one foot with the other foot and both arms held off the floor. The judges picked off the kids who toppled over.

The music speeded up. We skated faster.

"Shoot the duck!" the announcer hollered.

Marianne's hand touched the ground and a judge sent her to the benches.

The music went faster and we went faster, Elsie keeping up right beside me.

"Shoot the duck!"

We crouched down together, but both Elsie's feet shot out and she hit the cement.

Two boys and I ended up with the slips for free pop. Back at the rail, I offered mine to Elsie.

"No thanks," she said. "I'm going to be only a hundred and five pounds by seventh grade."

"Well, if you're going to give up that much padding," Jenny advised her, "you'd better stay out of the rinks."

At school the next day, Jimmy was sort of quiet around me. It was five minutes before the bell and half the class was at the back table where Jack and Jimmy were putting the finishing touches on a salt-and-flour map of Mexico.

"I wish I'd thought of a map for a project," I told Jimmy. "My mother has me dressing a doll in a festival costume and the sewing's a drag."

Jimmy barely shrugged in reply. He kept his head bent over the map and all I could see was his straight sandy hair. Leon muscled up to the table, pushing me and Jimmy apart. "My brother saw you at the rink last night," Leon said to me.

"I had a party."

"How come I didn't get invited?" he wanted to know.

"Because you're not a girl."

"Boys like parties, too," Jimmy said quietly.

Oh, I'd hurt his feelings. Jimmy and I had been friends since first grade. I moved around Leon and put my hand on Jimmy's shoulder. "Next year I'll have a party on Halloween and we'll go to the ghost house."

"Hey, all right," Leon said.

Jimmy looked up. "She didn't say *you*."

"Listen, wienie . . ."

The bell rang and Mrs. Lobb entered the room with her arms full of ditto sheets. She dumped them on her desk, took roll, and then stood in front of us for our complete attention. "Since this is the last week of the quarter, I've prepared tests to cover the material we've gone over this far. Starting tomorrow we'll have one or two tests a day.

"I don't want any surprises on your report cards, so, after I grade your tests, I will give them back to you. I suggest you take them home so your parents don't have any surprises, either."

Sharon's hand shot up. "Do you mean all the homework we did and all the papers we handed in aren't going to count?"

"I'll certainly take them into consideration and no one will get an A or a B if he or she hasn't completed the daily work."

Mrs. Lobb called on Jack. He must have had his hand up, too. "What about our social studies projects?"

"Oh, I forgot about that. Since you've worked on

those for more than two weeks, they will be a fourth of your grade. And, of course, your participation in music and P.E. will determine whether you get a satisfactory mark in those activities."

My hand went up. "Do you mean we don't get regular grades in P.E. and music?"

"You'll get satisfactory or unsatisfactory in the non-academic subjects."

I slid down in my seat. I was done for.

Mrs. Lobb looked around the classroom. "Are there any other questions? I want all this to be very clear. I don't want any of you taking a report card home and telling your parents you don't understand how you got your grades.

"Jimmy? You have a question?"

"It sounds to me like," Jimmy said, "we've done a pile of work for ten weeks for nothing."

She shook her head. "You wouldn't play a basketball tournament without practicing first, would you? Game scores and grades reflect your real ability. You could do all your lessons at home and still read below a sixth-grade level. Then you couldn't pass sixth-grade reading, could you?"

My face burned. Guess who?

"Any more questions? You all look so solemn. The tests simply go over the same work you've already done." She stood still a minute with her thumb pressed against her lips. She seemed to be trying to remember something.

"If you'll turn to page 41 in your arithmetic book, you'll find a review test you can practice on. The answers are in the back of the book. If you have any trouble with the problems, I'll help you."

She started for her desk and then turned back to us. "Oh, and don't forget to bring your social studies projects to school tomorrow. Jack and Jimmy can leave theirs on the back table. The rest of you can spread yours out on the front table."

I watched her sit down, pick up the ditto sheets by clumps, bang the edges on her desk to straighten the pages, and put them into her bottom drawer. When she was finished, she fished a key from her purse and locked the drawer. I took my arithmetic book slowly out of my desk.

Jack mumbled behind me, "What a rip-off."

He should complain. He can read. In fact, he spends all his spare time reading library books. He thinks it's fun!

Mother greeted me at the door with her usual big smile, which faded as soon as she saw my face. "Why, Helen, what's the matter."

"I'm flunking sixth grade, that's what's the matter."

After she'd pried every detail of Mrs. Lobb's announcements out of me, Mother squinted her eyes thoughtfully. "We'll wait to see how your report card turns out and then maybe I'll have to have a conference with Mrs. Lobb."

"I don't think you know Mrs. Lobb."

"Well," she said sharply, "I *do* know she isn't the only sixth-grade teacher in that school. Now come on, let's finish your Mexican doll since that's a fourth of your grade. I bought some glue for the hair."

Mrs. Lobb liked my doll, which amazed me. She fingered all the colored layers of the doll's skirt and said she made a costume similar to mine when she was a girl.

"The hems aren't very straight." I was leaning on the front table with the other kids and I was a little embarrassed by all her attention.

"Oh, that's all right. I'm sure I didn't do any better." She patted the doll's head. "Where did you get the hair?"

"My mother saved my hair when it was cut off this summer and I glued some of it on the doll. Since my hair's almost black, I thought it would work." Now I was really embarrassed.

"How ingenious," she said.

She moved on to the other projects. Dawn had brought a papier-mâché piñata in the shape of a donkey. "My dad's seen them in Mexico," Dawn explained. "And if

53

we want to save the piñata and break it the day before Christmas vacation, he'll fill it up with candy."

"That sounds like it would be fun," Mrs. Lobb agreed. "We could have a little festival."

Jimmy widened his eyes at me. What? A party in Mrs. Lobb's room???

Sharon had made a pizza. Mrs. Lobb broke off a chunk and ate it.

"The dough didn't get quite done," Sharon said.

Mrs. Lobb swallowed. "I see."

While we got down to reviewing our spelling, Mrs. Lobb put our project grades in her grade book, wrote out little slips with each student's name and mark, and handed them out to us. We compared our slips at recess. Sharon got a C. Jack, Jimmy, Dawn, and I all got As.

That was the good part of the week.

Way to Go!

On Tuesday we had tests in spelling and health. I didn't mind the spelling really. I knew I was going to flunk it. During most of the test, I wrote down the first three letters of a word and waited for Mrs. Lobb to go on to the next one. Unfortunately, since there were fifty words, that gave me a lot of time to be sitting up straight and smelling Warren. Why didn't he take a bath? I felt like giving him a hard punch.

Part of the health examination was putting the right numbers on a diagram of the digestive system. Down below the drawing were the numbers followed by words. I couldn't read all the words, but since I knew the digestive system by heart, I could figure most of them out.

When I wanted the number for the esophagus, I looked through all the words to find one that ended in *gus*. When I wanted the number for pancreas, I looked through all the words to find one that began with *pan*. I was so busy, it startled me when Mrs. Lobb asked us to hand our papers in because it was almost lunch time.

"But I'm not finished!" I said right out loud.

"Neither am I," added Warren. I almost liked him for a minute because he was the only other one in the room who wasn't done.

Mrs. Lobb frowned at us for not raising our hands, thought a minute, and then said, "Well, if you don't mind being at the end of the line, you can work until the lunch cart is ready to leave."

I worked like mad while the other kids filed into the hall to get their food. Jack poked me in the back to let me know when the last kid brought his tray into the classroom. I scribbled down an answer to the final question, slapped my paper on Mrs. Lobb's desk, and went for the lunch cart. The creamed chicken over mashed potatoes was cold, but I didn't care. I knew I wouldn't get a good grade on the test because I couldn't read all the directions. All I hoped was that I did enough to pass.

The next day was social studies. Twenty-five true-or-false statements. My fingers clawed at my head as I tried to guess the big words from the little words around them. I felt a little better when Mrs. Lobb returned our health papers. All my numbers on the digestive system were right and my grade was a D-plus.

Thursday was reading. Ten long gray paragraphs followed by questions. There wasn't a chance. Before school was out, we got our social studies tests back. Mine was an F, of course.

I handed it to my mother at the door of the house. "Here's another F. I got an F in spelling, and I know I got an F in reading today, so that makes three Fs and a D-plus. I might as well quit right now."

She looked quickly over the paper and then turned it face down on her desk and took in a breath. "All you can do, Helen, is your best. That's all anyone can do. When is your arithmetic exam?"

"Tomorrow." I headed for my room.

"You'll get an A for sure. Wait a minute. Don't you think we should go over some of the problems?"

"No," I told her from halfway up the stairs.

"But . . ." She started after me.

I beat her to my bedroom and closed my door.

Dinner was roast veal, new potatoes, and peas. I cut up my potatoes, poured gravy over them, and squished them into mush with my fork.

Dad watched me with annoyance. "If you don't

want your dinner, simply say 'no thank you.' "

I ate two peas.

He turned to Mother. "The Lindstroms are having some friends down to their cabin at Ocean Shores this weekend. Want to go?"

"I don't know. When are they leaving?"

"Friday evening and coming back Sunday." He looked at me. "Could you stay with Louise?"

"Sure."

"There's no way I can be gone the whole weekend," Mother put in quickly. "Helen's having tests."

"My last test is tomorrow and I won't have any homework this weekend because it's the end of the quarter." I carefully cut the outside edge off a slice of my meat.

"Helen!" Mother said. "There isn't any fat on veal."

"Don't get mad at me just because you don't want to go to Ocean Shores," I told her.

"That has nothing to do with it. Veal's expensive."

Dad was watching Mother closely. "You have a husband, too—not only a daughter."

"I'm aware of that, Fred, but Helen has a special problem."

Dad pushed back his chair. "Maybe it's time we let the school take care of that. It doesn't seem to me like all your work is having much success."

"How can you say that?" Mother cried out. "Helen and I try so hard."

"I'm saying," Dad said quietly, "if one way isn't doing the job, perhaps it's time to try another."

Mother pushed her chair back, too. Her chin was jutted forward. "Are you going to want some dessert?"

"No, thank you," Dad said.

Before I went to bed that night, I crawled into my closet to check on my rubber boot. I took the ten dollars out of the toe and pulled out my firecrackers, two chasers and one M70. Not very much left out of the pile Uncle Leo bought me.

I fingered the firecrackers for a little while, then put them away, and crawled into bed to imagine Uncle Leo sending me a computer. A new experimental one that could beam out holograms.

I devised a space game for it that didn't need joy sticks. The players stood inside the hologram and shot the zooming invaders with pop guns. When Uncle Leo came at Christmas and saw my game, he was so impressed he set up a company with me to sell it. I was so busy keeping track of the orders for the company I didn't have time to go to school. A tutor came two hours a day to teach me my lessons.

I hired Louise to wrap the games for mailing. And her brother Christian drove the truck to the post office. Jimmy and Jack took phone orders. We got interviewed on TV as the first company run by sixth-graders.

When I turned over to look at my clock, it was twelve-thirty. I thought I'd better save the rest of my adventure for the next night and go to sleep so I could do well in my arithmetic test. School, ugh.

The arithmetic test Mrs. Lobb passed out was three pages long. The first page was multiplication of decimals. I started doing the problems at a good clip, wrinkling my face up every once in a while to try to get the smell of Warren out of my nose.

"Hel. Hel. Ssss, Helen."

I looked over at Leon. He held the edge of his paper up and pointed to the five numbers he had written below the third problem. I raised four fingers, Leon nodded, and put the decimal point after the fourth number, counting from the left.

I shook my head and motioned my index finger to the right. Leon nodded again, erased the decimal point, and put it in the correct place.

"What are you two doing?" Mrs. Lobb said behind us.

My heart stopped.

"I asked you what you were doing?" she repeated.

"I—I—I—," Leon stuttered. "We—I—Just checking an answer."

"Let me have your paper."

Leon handed her his paper.

"Let me have yours, Helen."

I handed her mine.

She marched up to the front of the room and threw both of the papers in the wastebasket. The room was as silent as death. I sat watching the classroom clock, not seeing any of its numbers, while the hour clicked away.

Lunch time came. I might as well have eaten sawdust. Reading time came. Mrs. Lobb sat at her desk checking arithmetic answers. I stared at my book, not even trying the questions at the end of the chapter. Instead, I imagined all the laughing and yelling kids in my class climbing on the junior high bus while I walked alone to the little elementary school for another year.

Jack poked me. "My pencil broke. You got an extra one?"

"Take mine." I flipped it back to him. It landed on the floor and I got up to get it.

"Helen, what are you doing?" Mrs. Lobb demanded.

"Nothing." I dropped the pencil on Jack's desk and sat back down.

"What do you mean 'nothing?' Why were you playing with Jack's pencil?"

"I wasn't playing."

She rose from her chair. "Have you finished all your questions?"

"I haven't started."

Her lips pulled tight across her teeth in exasperation. "I think you'd better move to the back of the room away from so many boys."

"Wait a minute," Jack said. "I asked Helen for a pencil."

She looked at him coldly. "Did you raise your hand? Helen, I want you to move."

I took my arithmetic book out slowly and placed it on my lap. Next, I took my health book out slowly.

Mrs. Lobb put her hands on her hips. "Will you please empty your desk *fast!*"

"All right." I shot my hand into my desk and swooped a pile of books and Pee Chees to the floor. Stuck my hand in again and dumped pencils, pens, and ruler on top of them.

"Way to go, Helen!" Jimmy yelled.

The kids laughed. Warren twisted around to watch the action, and Leon moved out of the way as I swished out the last of my crumpled papers and gum wrappers.

Mrs. Lobb stood in front of me, swelling up like a huge toad. "You pick that mess up immediately, young lady."

I picked up two of my books. Anyway, I'd get away from Warren's stinky feet. "Where am I supposed to sit?"

"Sit in the very back seat. Right there behind Jimmy."

I turned around quick to look into Jimmy's grinning face.

Before the class had settled down, the school secretary came in to give Mrs. Lobb a message. The secretary took a fast glance around the room, which made Mrs. Lobb's face turn red. Mrs. Lobb got back at us later in the afternoon by substituting sit-up exercises for our usual game in P.E.

After school Mother forgot to be cheerful when I handed her my yellow discipline slip. "Oh, no, we aren't starting *this* again!" she wailed.

Red Eye

"What did your mom say about the discipline slip?" Louise asked me, through a mouthful of pie crust. We were sitting at the kitchen table helping her mother make dinner. I was peeling carrots and Louise was tearing spinach leaves. Her mother was taking a rhubarb pie out of the oven.

Whenever Mrs. Martin makes crust, she flattens the extra dough into little circles, sprinkles them with cinnamon and sugar, and bakes them beside the pie. Louise and I usually hover around until they're done. With so many kids in the family, whoever gets to the cookies first eats them all up.

Mrs. Martin spread a section of newspaper on the counter and placed the hot, bubbling pie on top of it. "A discipline slip! Helen, a pretty girl like you." She gave Louise a stern look. "You better not come home with a discipline slip."

"Mama, don't yell at me. Mr. Marshall doesn't even hand out discipline slips. Anyway, they're no big thing. They just say, 'We are sorry you broke this rule,' and then one of the hundred rules has a check after it."

Mrs. Martin's black eyes rounded. "There are a hundred rules on the slip?"

Louise shook her head. The light caught on her tiny blue earrings, making them sparkle. "No, about ten, but there's a space below where the teachers can write in anything else they decide is evil."

Mrs. Martin took a large glass casserole dish of lasagna out of the refrigerator, placed it in the oven, and turned to concentrate on me. "So what did you do?"

"I helped a boy with his math test and then I gave another boy a pencil when he broke his, only the teacher didn't know it was my pencil. She thought I was playing with his."

"You didn't explain to her?" Mrs. Martin asked.

"Mama, you can't explain to a teacher like that." Louise wiped her hands on the dish towel we were sharing. "The stuff for the salad is all finished. Can we go play with the rabbits now?"

Christian wandered into the kitchen and helped himself to the three crust cookies that were left on a plate in front of Louise. Louise snatched the plate away too late. "Pig," she told him.

"Well, how many have you eaten?" He stuffed a cookie in his mouth. "Ma, I've got a chance to work the noon shift Monday, O.K.?"

"Monday is school," Mrs. Martin said.

He stuffed another cookie in. "Missing one day won't make any difference."

"Three Ds will let you graduate?"

"That's correct. That's all I need." He threw the last cookie in the air and caught it in his mouth.

"All right. This one last time. But not again until you graduate. School comes first."

"School makes me puke," Christian said, and walked out of the kitchen.

I loved that. School makes me puke, too.

"It must be neat to have Christian for a big brother," I said to Louise, as she pulled Red Eye out of his cage.

"Most of the time it is. Especially when he takes me places." She set the rabbit in the grass. He stretched out his front legs to reach for a chunk of clover and then brought his back legs up with a hop.

French Lops are huge brown bunnies. They're about as big as a cocker spaniel, with ears that hang down like a spaniel, too. My favorite is Bear, but all of them aren't as nice as he is. Red Eye will scratch you if he doesn't know your scent. Louise can be real sneaky about giving kids she hates a carrot to feed Red Eye.

Her brothers and sisters are like that, too. They have a rowdy sense of humor. When you eat dinner at their house, one will pass you a plate of celery sticks and then no one at the table will say a word while you try to crunch down the celery in total silence.

After Louise and I finished the dinner dishes that Friday night, Christian took us to a horror movie. Actually, he let us off in front of the Lynn Four Plex theaters and came back to get us. He did that Saturday night, too. Carole wanted to come, but fortunately her mother thought it would be too far past her bedtime.

I spent Uncle Leo's ten dollars. If I'd asked Mother for some money she would have insisted on knowing which movie we were going to see. Christian was late picking us up Saturday night. While we waited for him, we huddled against the ticket booth trying to stay clear of the rain.

"Where'd your mom go this weekend?" Louise asked me.

"To Ocean Shores."

"That's a neat resort. She's lucky."

I pulled the hood of my jacket tighter around my face. The Liza Minnelli haircut didn't keep my head very warm.

"My folks hardly go anywhere," Louise added.

"My mother would like it if she didn't. She gets all shook up when she has to go out with Dad's customers."

Louise covered her taffy-colored hair with her hands to protect it from the blowing rain. "Why? She's pretty."

"She doesn't think so. She's always worrying that she won't be wearing the right thing or say the right thing. Her dad died when she was seven and her mother sold dresses at Penney's, but she didn't make much. Mother and Uncle Leo went to work before they got through high school. It doesn't seem to bother him, but Mother still thinks she's out of it."

"You're lucky your uncle is loaded."

I know I am. Uncle Leo sells Kabota tractors all over the Northwest. It's like my birthday every time he comes to visit us in Brier.

"Finally, Christian!" Louise moved out toward his oncoming car. He had a girl in the front seat, so Louise and I had to crouch on the floor behind them riding home.

"You were late enough," Louise complained to him.

"Don't knock it," Christian told her. "You're getting a free ride."

Louise didn't say any more. She knows a good thing.

Sunday I had to go back home. It was quiet at my house. As soon as Mother was unpacked, she got into one of her caftans, settled on the davenport with a cup of tea, and told me to bring my reading book so I could practice with her. I obeyed because I had to, but I didn't see what the point was. I was already failing.

"You must keep trying," she insisted.

I kept trying, for all the good it did me. On my report card, I got Fs in reading, spelling, and social studies, a D-plus in health, a C in arithmetic, and Ss in the rest of the subjects, except for citizenship which was a U. Under "Comments" Mrs. Lobb had written, "In danger of failing sixth grade."

My mother looked over my card with a jutted chin and had Mr. Douglas on the phone so fast it must have made the secretary dizzy. She got an appointment for her and my dad the very next afternoon. Mr. Douglas told Mother to bring me along.

I'd never been to a conference before and I sat in the office beside my parents with a trickle of sweat sliding down the inside of my white blouse to the waist of the freshly ironed yellow skirt that Grandma had made for me. Mr. Douglas came in after the school buses had pulled out. Mrs. Lobb was with him, yuck.

They sat down with us at the round table. Mr. Douglas introduced my mother and dad to Mrs. Lobb. He knows my parents very well. Since my first grade year, in fact.

"Well, let's see if we can finally find some resolutions to Helen's problems," Mr. Douglas started out.

My mother gave him a wary look. I knew she didn't want anything to do with his idea of a resolution. He meant my going into a special class for dumb kids.

I slumped down in my seat. The whole thing made me sick. Mother jabbed me in the side. I sat up in my seat.

"The first thing I'd like to understand is Helen's arithmetic grade." Mother always uses my arithmetic grade to prove how smart I am. "I am aware that Helen helped a boy during his math test and we have talked with her about how wrong that was."

Mrs. Lobb nodded.

"But," my mother went on, "I don't understand how that can penalize her two whole grades on a quarter report card."

Mr. Douglas motioned to Mrs. Lobb to explain that one.

"If Helen tells a student an answer during a test," Mrs. Lobb said, "I have no way of knowing how much learning that student has acquired."

"We agree with you that Helen behaved incorrectly. We aren't disputing her U in citizenship. What I don't understand is how Helen can receive a C in arithmetic."

"But if Helen cheats on a test, I can't very well use the results of that test, now can I?" Mrs. Lobb replied sharply.

"No, but you surely have ways of knowing how capable Helen is in arithmetic without using the results of one test, don't you?" Mother's voice was equally sharp and Dad placed his hand on her shoulder. She shot him an exasperated glance.

Mr. Douglas moved in. "We're talking, after all, about a quarter report. We'll assume that Helen will know better than to discuss answers during her semester test. Is that right, Helen?"

I nodded obediently.

"Now about Helen's other grades," he prompted Mrs. Lobb.

"Yes." She took up her grade book. "The only other academic subject in which Helen obtained a passing mark was health, and that leaves her in danger of failing sixth grade."

"May I go to the lavatory?" I asked.

Dad started to say O.K., but Mother was quicker. "You'll be able to wait until we're finished in here," she told me.

Mrs. Lobb went on. "Helen very obviously has a reading problem."

"We're aware of that." Mother said. "But are you telling me all the hours she put in on her homework count for nothing?"

Mr. Douglas shifted in his seat. He must have heard Mother's arguments before.

"I agree Helen is a hard worker *when* she attends to

business," Mrs. Lobb answered. "However, there's no way I know of that a student who reads on a second- or third-grade level can pass in a regular sixth grade."

I slid down in my chair again and concentrated on the blue stripes on my Nike's. Second-grade level!

"We've been working with Helen at home. Have you worked with her at school?" Mother asked Mrs. Lobb.

"I work with *thirty* students," Mrs. Lobb replied.

"Have you ever once helped Helen individually?" Mother insisted.

"I have a whole classroom to attend to."

"Yes, I've heard you've had some difficulty with that." Mother looked her straight in the eyes. "Perhaps if you didn't leave your classroom so often . . ."

Oh, oh. I was going to get blamed for Sharon Hinkler's big mouth.

"Ummmm," Mr. Douglas got everyone's attention. "I know we've discussed this before, but I really feel we should consider another educational alternative for Helen. Why don't we ask the school psychologist to test her and make some recommendations."

Before Dad could agree, Mother said. "We've had Helen tested at the University of Washington. The psychologist there told us Helen has above-average intelligence."

"I'm sure she has." Mr. Douglas nodded. "Many LD students do, but that doesn't mean they can survive in

72

the school system without a special program."

Mother's face turned rock hard. "I think what Helen needs is a different teacher. Instead of more testing, I would like to request that she be moved into Mr. Marshall's room."

Mr. Douglas sighed, gathered up the papers, and put them back in my file. "Well, then, let's wait until the end of the semester to see how Helen does. We can discuss a transfer at that time if it seems appropriate."

Mrs. Lobb rose from her seat. She was steaming. Dad shook hands with Mr. Douglas and Mother picked up her purse. "We'll stop at the lavatory for you," she said to me.

Out in the parking lot, my parents didn't speak to each other while they got in the car and Dad turned on the ignition. "What does LD mean?" I asked from the back seat.

"Learning disabled," Dad said.

Learning disabled? I felt like a cripple.

The next morning I couldn't get out of bed. I was able to wobble to the bathroom and back and that was it. After Mother took my temperature, Dad came in and stroked my forehead.

"I wish I could make your life easier, Helen." He looked so sad I was afraid he might cry.

There were angry voices downstairs before he left for work. As the front door opened, his words traveled up the stairs. "At the next conference we go to, I'm going to have *my* say."

Being in a dumb room or being dumb in a regular room, what difference did it make? I turned over on my stomach to wait for the puking to begin.

Healing Stones

I threw up all night. In the morning Mother changed my sheets again, put a large bath towel beside my pillow, a clean pan on the floor beside my bed, and then waited nervously for the doctor's office to open. On the dot of nine, she went downstairs to call him.

She brought back up some apple juice and told me the doctor had said to keep me warm, feed me fluids, and call him again if the vomiting persisted. It persisted. She bundled me up and took me into the office the next day for his first appointment.

The doctor peered in my ears, poked down my throat, thumped me front and back, said, "Hmmm," and "Well,

I think she's caught the bug that's going around. I'll give her something to settle her stomach. Keep her quiet until it runs its course."

"When do you think Helen will be well enough to return to school?" Mother asked the doctor.

"Oh, when she feels up to it."

That would be about never, I thought.

I took the stomach medicine as soon as I got home. It was some syrupy stuff that tasted like mouthwash. It worked, though. By the time Mother had lunch and was ready to go grocery shopping, the rolling, pukey feeling had disappeared.

I curled up on the davenport to watch TV. Before "General Hospital" was over, she was back and putting the groceries away in the kitchen. "Do you want to try some apple juice now?" she asked, coming into the living room with her hands behind her.

"No!" I'd thrown up every glass she'd given me. I wasn't going to start again.

"Then I've got something for you." She brought out two packages from behind her back and sat down beside me with a happy smile on her face. Mother loves to give presents.

The first one was a small camera. "It was on sale at Safeway," she told me. "At PTA they said all the sixth-graders go up to Orcas Island for a week in the spring. You learn about fish and forestry and the history of the

San Juans. So I thought you'd like to take pictures on your trip."

"That's neat," I said. I liked having a camera even though I was too tired to be interested in the life cycle of the salmon.

"Open the other package," she said eagerly.

I did. There were three hard baseballs in the bottom of the sack. "These are great. How did you think of them?" I didn't tell her we can only play softball in sixth grade. I carried my presents upstairs and settled down in bed for a nap.

When I heard Dad come home, I wobbled down to eat a little fruit salad. The asparagus and meat smelled awful. Mother held a slice of pot roast toward me. "Do you want to try a small piece?"

"No." I backed away from the smell.

"Don't push her!" Dad's voice was harsh.

Mother looked at him, surprised. Her hand holding the serving fork wilted down to the platter.

After dinner Dad and I played checkers up in my room until I got sleepy again. I felt pretty good in the morning. But when Mother came in all rise and shine, I squeaked out a weak, little hello.

A couple of mornings later, I felt even better because I heard Uncle Leo downstairs. I threw the covers off and was halfway out of my bed . . . Whoops! How was I going to work this? School hadn't started yet.

I waited fifteen minutes until Uncle Leo bounded up the steps. "Hi, sweetie pie," he said at my door. "Feel good enough for me to come in?"

"Sure," I said, throwing back my covers like it was the first time that morning. "I can probably get up now."

"If you can be up this early, maybe you'd better go to school," Mother said from behind Uncle Leo.

"Ah, have a heart, Emily," he told her. "I hardly ever see the kid and I won't be here for Christmas."

I shoved my feet in my slippers. "You won't be here for Christmas! Why not?"

"Your grandmother's heart's giving her trouble again. I think I'd better stay with her."

"Grandma isn't coming, either? What kind of a Christmas will this be?"

Uncle Leo put his arm around me and walked me to the bathroom. "We'll have Christmas today. After you brush your teeth, come on down and I'll make you some of my de-licious pancakes."

I put my hand on my stomach. "I don't know . . ."

But I was able to eat three of Uncle Leo's pancakes. "This is the only thing that's tasted good all week," I told him, swirling the last bite around in the syrup left on my plate.

Uncle Leo smiled. "And we'll go to lunch at Gretchen's of Course."

"Oh, I just love to eat at Gretchen's of Course!"

Mother got up from her chair and started picking up the plates. "Well, enjoy yourself today because you're going back to school for sure on Monday."

I wrinkled my nose at Uncle Leo.

The first place Uncle Leo and I stopped was at a jewelry store in the University District. I followed him in, not really knowing what we were there for. When the saleslady asked if she could help us, Uncle Leo said, "Ah, yes, I think we want some ears pierced and some earrings to go with them."

What???

"This young lady?" She peered down at me for such a long time I thought she was seeing all of my insides. She had black hair sleeked into a bun at the side of her neck. She wore dangling violet earrings, amethysts I learned later, that matched her violet eyes. She was as old as Mrs. Lobb, but instead of making me feel cold around her she made me warm, I think.

She reached out for my hand, led me behind a counter, and sat me on a stool. While I waited for her to put a gold post in a gunlike tool, I scrinched my shoulders toward Uncle Leo, who was standing beside me. "Mother's going to be mad."

"She'll get over it," Uncle Leo said.

The gun didn't really hurt. There were two hot pinches and then it was done. "Rotate the posts twice a day and clean around them with alcohol until your ears heal." The saleslady took my hand again. "Now let's go over and see which stones will do you the most good."

Uncle Leo and I leaned over a glass counter and surveyed the trays of earrings the lady put in front of us. There were so many pretty ones I didn't know how to choose. "Maybe that one," I suggested, pointing to a round silver pair with black centers. They didn't look too expensive. I didn't want to be piggy about Uncle Leo's gift.

The lady shook her head, swinging her earrings back and forth. "Onyx? No, not for you. They'd give you bad dreams. I think maybe topaz." She picked up two tiny gold flowers with gleaming yellow centers.

I looked questioningly at Uncle Leo.

"Well, do you like them?" he asked.

"They're beautiful, but are they too expensive?"

"You're not supposed to worry about the cost of presents."

I turned back to the lady. "I love them."

She smiled. "Of course. Topaz is the symbol of the sun. It takes away depression."

I had a feeling she knew.

"How about these, too?" Uncle Leo pointed to some sky blue stones.

"Turquoise?" She stood with her head bowed a minute, then raised it, and put a finger beside her soft cheek. "I think jade would be better."

She brought out another tray and took up a pair of small stones that were the color of green apples in early summer. She held them against the back of my hand. "What do you think?" she asked Uncle Leo.

"They look like they belong to her, all right."

She turned my hand over, placed the earrings inside. "Their healing radiations will benefit your sight."

Leaving the jewelry store, with the two satin boxes tucked safely in my purse, I said to my uncle, "She was the strangest lady I ever met."

Gretchen's of Course is on the balcony of Mario's, a clothing shop on Sixth Avenue in Seattle. You walk by glass partitions to select your food. The baked salmon, rice, and salad were easy, but I never know what to choose when I get to the dessert section. Uncle Leo decided on pecan pie. I finally settled on blueberry crunch slopped over with real whipped cream.

We sat at a table overlooking the counters of men's sweaters and poles of women's dresses standing on the floor below. Uncle Leo thought he might buy one of the navy corduroy jackets before we left the store.

"I wish . . ."

Uncle Leo looked up from his bite of salmon and

rice. His eyes are bluer than Mother's and when he pays attention to you, he really focuses in. Sometimes I like it. Sometimes it makes me shy.

"What do you wish?" he prompted me.

"I wish I never had to go to school again."

"That bad, eh? What happened that made it worse than it usually is for you?"

So while we ate our lunch I poured out all my misery over being dumb in reading and poured out all my worry over Mother's accusing Mrs. Lobb of leaving the class-room. "Mrs. Lobb will think I told on her," I explained to Uncle Leo.

Uncle Leo pushed his empty dinner dish away and slid his pie plate closer. "Has she ever been mean to any of you?"

"No, she hasn't been exactly mean. I don't think she likes kids very well. Or she expects them not to act like kids."

"Well, you've given her a week to cool down," he said, sipping the coffee from his glass mug. "By Monday she may pretty well have forgotten what happened in the conference."

I slowly smashed the whipped cream until it reached all the edges of the blueberry juice. I wasn't so sure Mrs. Lobb would forget.

"Do you know what I used to do when I was a kid

and I was scared my mother had found out what I'd done?"

"No, what?" I asked him.

"I used to say to myself, 'All she can do is kill me.' That used to make me real brave and I'd walk right in the house saying to myself, 'She can only kill me.' "

I tried it out with a little shrug. "Sixth grade can only kill me."

False Alarm

Mother wasn't too mad about my ears. She said that she would have preferred that I had waited to pierce them until I was at least fourteen, but she thought the earrings were very tasteful. I told her the saleslady said topaz makes your depression go away.

"Topaz!" Mother exclaimed. "Leo, are these real stones?"

I quickly put them back in their boxes and disappeared upstairs, letting Uncle Leo handle Mother.

He left the next morning, which was Sunday. After lunch I went over to the Martins' garage sale with the two dollars Dad gave me to spend. I wandered around in the crowd until I found a black sleeveless T-shirt of Christian's that had white skulls printed on it.

Louise was being cashier at a table in front of the garage doors. I paid her fifty cents for the shirt and asked her if that old alarm clock on the tool shelf really worked.

"Sure," she said. "We just don't need it any more because we have electric ones."

"Do you have a plastic sack to put it in?"

Louise got one from her kitchen. I gave her another fifty cents and left for home. There's a big fir tree in our front yard. I stuck the plastic sack deep in its branches before I went into the house.

The next morning I came down to breakfast in my fuzz jeans and white turtleneck sweater with Christian's T-shirt pulled on top.

"Helen," Mother said, "you are not wearing that outfit to school."

Dad looked up from his scrambled eggs. "I think she looks pretty cute."

Mother served me my eggs in pursed-lip silence.

After she managed a begrudging kiss good-bye and had closed the front door, I walked across the wet grass to the fir tree and took out the alarm clock. There was a cold rain falling so I huddled against the branches while I set and wound the clock, set the alarm for one-thirty, and gave the alarm key one turn. I tucked the clock up inside my jacket where I could hold it with my arm, and took off for Louise's.

Walking to school beside me, Louise noticed the gold posts in my ears. "You did it!" she cried. "You got your ears pierced."

When I went into the classroom, Sharon and Marianne noticed them, too. "Where'd you have it done?" Marianne asked.

"In the U District," I told her. Mrs. Lobb wasn't in the room yet so I eased over to my seat, dropped my reading book on my desk, took out a couple sheets of paper, eased to the back wastebasket, slipped the clock into the basket, dropped the papers on top, and hung up my jacket.

"Wicked shirt," Jimmy said when I sat back down.

Mrs. Lobb came in about five minutes later. I took my excuse up to her desk. She did a double take on the skulls, but didn't say anything to me.

At lunch recess we couldn't play any games because of the rain. Louise and I stood under the covered area talking about how much her family made on the garage sale and how she wished she'd thought of wearing Christian's shirt. "I could have got it off him for free," she said.

Mrs. Lobb finished up *Old Yeller* and had us take out our reading books. She read the first two paragraphs of a story about spaceships and then called on students

86

to read the following paragraphs. She was picking kids sitting in my row. I had one finger in place on the page and my eyes on the big hand of the classroom clock as it inched down toward one-thirty.

Even I jumped. I didn't realize the alarm would make such an awful noise in the metal wastebasket.

"Line up! Line up!" Mrs. Lobb commanded.

"No, wait . . ." Jack's red head turned toward the back of the room.

"I said to line up. Now do it quickly. All of you."

The clanging stopped, leaving the room in shocking silence. Everyone was lined up beside the front blackboard, except Sharon. She was trying to explain to Mrs. Lobb that the alarm wasn't the fire drill bell.

"Will you please get in place, miss. I don't need you to tell me how to run my classroom." Mrs. Lobb waved us out the door.

"What an idiot," Jimmy mumbled behind me, as she marched us out to the empty field.

We shivered in the rain until Mrs. Lobb gave it up and marched us in again. When we were quietly seated, she pushed the intercom button to the office.

"Yes?" we heard the secretary say.

"An alarm went off in my room. Can you tell me what it was for?"

There were a few minutes of silence until the secretary came back on. "I can't see anything lit up on the board here. I'll have the janitor check the wires."

Lucky for me the janitor didn't get to our room before the end of the day. And lucky for me, Mrs. Lobb had never gone through a fire drill in our school. I managed to get the clock out of the wastebasket when she dismissed us. Jack saw me, but I didn't have to worry about him. The next day I read aloud fine because I had every paragraph in the story memorized.

After school Wednesday, I stood around the Martins' kitchen, watching them prepare pumpkin pies and mince pies and cranberry sauce. We were having such a small Thanksgiving dinner at our house without Uncle Leo or Grandma that I wished I could eat with Louise. It seems weird to me that our family has more money than Louise's, but they have more food.

The first weeks of December were massively boring at school. Mother made me study and study and I still got Fs and Fs. Things picked up the week before Christmas vacation, though, when the sixth-grade classes got rowdy. Mr. Douglas came on the intercom to give us a talk about being a model for the younger kids. His talk didn't make any difference, of course.

Dawn brought her donkey piñata back to school. It was chock full of candy. We all gathered around to poke at it. Mrs. Lobb put it in her closet, saying she'd keep it there until we were ready for it on Friday. Dawn told her that sometimes there were firecrackers at Mexican celebrations. Mrs. Lobb said that was interesting, but there wouldn't be any at ours.

I licked my lips. We'd see about that.

On Friday, excitement rippled through the sixth-grade unit like fire. Most of Mr. Marshall's kids were milling in the hall trying on costumes. Their room was having Christmas plays and they invited us in to see them. Mrs. Lobb asked their room to join us in breaking the piñata.

She tried to make us do social studies and spelling first. At ten o'clock, after many threats that if we didn't settle down she was going to cancel everything, we were ready to march next door and see the plays. The kids had written them so they were pretty dumb, but it was fun anyway.

When the plays were over, we all marched back to our room for the Mexican festival, which consisted of blindfolded students wacking at the piñata with a broomstick. Jimmy and Warren had hung the donkey from one of the lights in the ceiling while the rest of us were out.

Sharon was blindfolded first and giggled through her turn. Jenny barely ticked the donkey. Leon completely missed it and Mrs. Lobb had to make Jimmy stop hooting. Diane bammed it a good one, splitting the donkey's stomach. Marianne spun it around and we could see the candy hanging in the crack.

Finally, since it was getting near lunch time, Mrs.

Lobb said we'd have to hit the piñata without the blind-fold. Jack jumped up to announce that he would do it. He got the baseball bat from the closet and swung with all his force. The donkey flew across the room, spraying its insides down the wall.

Sixty kids dived for the candy. I was on the bottom of the heap with Leon. I got ten pieces of candy, jabs in the ribs, and feet on my back. I could hear Mrs. Lobb crying, "Everybody up! Everybody up!"

One by one, Mr. Marshall pulled the kids to their feet. When I was free to get off the floor, I saw Leon holding his hand in front of his nose while blood dripped through his fingers. Our classroom door opened and Mrs. Lobb turned pale. It was only the cook wanting to know if our unit was ready for lunch. Mrs. Lobb said we would be in a minute. Mr. Marshall led Leon into the boys' lavatory to stop up his bloody nose.

During recess we girls stood under the covered area staring at the thick flakes of snow that were drifting down and melting into the ground. "Only three more hours to go," Jenny said.

Stacy wiggled back and forth trying to keep warm. "I wish we could go right now instead of sitting through that wacko music assembly."

"Actually, nobody would miss us if we left," Louise said.

I took my chaser out of one jacket pocket and matches

out of the other. Diane watched me. "Way to go!" She whistled.

I lit the firecracker and tossed it toward the classroom units. It hissed and crackled its jerky way up the concrete path. We followed after it, joined by the boys.

Mrs. Lobb and Miss Jewell came out of the faculty room. The crowd backed away as the chaser met the teachers on the walk between the buildings. Miss Jewell yelped. Mrs. Lobb's eyes narrowed as she searched through the dwindling group. Dumb me, I still had the matches in my hand.

Before I could get rid of them, Mrs. Lobb snatched me by the shoulder and dragged me into the office, her lips in a thin, straight line. She plunked me down in an office chair and announced to Mr. Douglas in a loud voice that she'd about had it with me. Mr. Douglas said he'd about had it with *all* the sixth-graders.

Discipline Slips

Mr. Douglas told me to wait for him in his office while he started the Christmas assembly. When he came back he carefully closed the door, sat down in his tilt-back chair, and said, "Now then, young lady, what are we going to do with you?"

I could only stare at him. What was there to say? He sighed, pulled his discipline box toward him on the desk, and took out my card. Or cards, since mine were stapled together in a fat lump.

"How many discipline slips have you had this year?"

"One," I told him.

"One?" He gave me a sharp look.

I turned up my hands. "One's all she's given me."

The punishments get harder with each slip. For the second one, you get thirty minutes' detention and your parents called. On the fifth, you get at least a three-day suspension.

Mr. Douglas reached for his phone. I concentrated on the wet snow swirling outside the office window while he told my mother I shot off a firecracker near the faculty room and endangered two of the teachers who were coming out the door. Principals always make what you do sound as bad as possible. He did the same thing in the lecture he gave me.

As soon as the chaser had zipped near the teachers, I had been scared it might hit their legs and I told Mr. Douglas this. And I told him I didn't set the firecracker off near the faculty room. It had just traveled there.

But he used what I said to explain and explain to me all the terrible things the chaser might have done. Like run in the midst of kindergarteners and put out one of their eyes or burn a teacher so badly she would have had to go to the hospital. Or me, it could have blown off my fingers. "And," he concluded, "isn't that kind of firecracker illegal?"

"Not on the Tulalip Indian reservation," I said.

He sat up very straight in his chair. Like a judge. "Do your parents take you there to buy illegal fireworks?"

"No, my Uncle Leo did, and they *aren't illegal* on the reservation." I didn't mean to sound smart, but I was getting all worn out from his exaggerations.

He eyed me coldly. "Helen, I think you're old enough to understand that you've used up all the goodwill in this school, and I've accommodated your mother far beyond what my professional judgment would decree. Now, today you'll stay in the office after school until I'm ready to leave, *but,* and you better remember this *but,* the next time you act out in this school we're going to have a conference with your parents and it's going to include more personnel than just your teacher and me. Do you understand?"

I didn't understand all of it, but I had the general idea, so I nodded obediently.

He left for the assembly, and I shifted around on my hard chair wondering what Miss Sleek would think when I didn't show up for the sixth-grade chorus. There was nothing to do for an hour but watch the snow and then watch the kids scream out of the gym and dash down the street. At four o'clock, when only the janitor was left in the school, Mr. Douglas put on his overcoat and said I could go home. I tried to say Merry Christmas to him as I went out the office door, but he was too busy switching off the lights to hear my shaky voice.

After I picked up my jacket, I stood in the middle of our empty classroom. It smelled of banana skins and orange peelings. The stripped bulletin boards prickled with broken staples, the floor was strewn with crumpled paper, the wastebaskets overflowed with crepe streamers and smashed red and green clay ornaments.

I felt so depressed the thought of getting my reading book out of my desk dragged my shoulders down. What was the use? I couldn't read. I couldn't memorize my whole reading book and social studies book and health book. I couldn't even learn twenty sixth-grade spelling words.

I coughed out a feeble laugh. What I knew how to do was set off firecrackers. I really and truly hadn't meant to hurt anybody. It made me feel bad that Mr. Douglas seemed to think I did.

The janitor's broom moved through the classroom door before he did. "How come you're still here?" he asked.

"I have to get my books," I told him. I might as well. It was easier than being brought back to school by a mad mother.

She met me at the door with her hand out. I put the discipline slip in it and followed her in for the next pounding. She screamed around a long time, mostly blaming her brother, Uncle Leo.

My father kept it short. He said I was eleven years old and should know better than to set off firecrackers at school. They both decided I'd be restricted to the house until Christmas Eve. "And that will give you plenty of time to concentrate on your studies," Mother added. I went to bed thinking this was some way to start a vacation.

For five days I worked on my reading, I worked on my health, and I worked on my social studies. I hated having Mother teach me. She made me practice the same way over and over and it never did any good. Finally, Christmas Eve came and ended the restriction.

I went to church with the Martins. Catholic churches are so beautiful on Easter and Christmas—I always get myself invited. On Easter there's the fragrance of the heavy white lilies and on Christmas there's the stained-glass windows lighted to show Mary holding the Christ child. And the chimes. I love the chimes.

It was snowing again when we came out of the church. This time it was sticking. Christian said if I brought my sled over the next day, he'd pull it with his car on the empty property behind their place. Louise said she'd come to get me after they opened their presents.

I had a stack of gifts under the tree. Christmas morning is totally great at my house. In fact I got so many presents—albums, gloves, sweaters, perfume, *and* my own stereo—that I put my new clothes away before Louise showed up. I had given Dad a chess set and he was a little disappointed that I was taking off before we had a chance to play a game. "We'll play as soon as I get back from sledding," I promised.

Louise wasn't too anxious to leave once she saw my stereo. I pushed her out the door, telling her we'd have plenty of time to listen to records after the snow melted. "Now be careful, you two," Mother called after us. She was lucky she didn't know we were sledding behind a car.

It has always seemed funny to me that my mother worries about every little thing I do and, just as she fears, I get in trouble, I break my arm, and I slice off the end of my finger. Louise's mom is too busy to worry, and her kids hardly ever get hurt.

When Louise and I reached the vacant lot with my sled, we found Christian tying a long, thick rope to the back of his car. Carole was hovering around him all decked out in furry mittens and a furry hat. "You got those for Christmas?" I asked her.

She turned to me, her eyes shining in her cold, pink face. "Yes, from Mom. And look what Dad gave me." She pulled off a mitten and held out a finger with a delicate silver ring and blue stone. "It's a lapis."

"It's sure pretty," I told her.

Christian stood up. "O.K. We're ready. Who's first?"

"We are," Louise said.

"Me," Carole said.

"My sled's big enough for all of us." I sat down and picked up the steering ropes, Carole climbed on behind me, and Louise got on in back.

Christian eased the car into gear and started a slow circle around the property. Carole held on tight and Christian kept his head out the window, checking the path of the sled as we went round and round. Twice Christian surprised us by gunning the car on a curve and tumbling us into the snow. The third time, I guided the sled in his wake and he couldn't slip us off. We rode until Christian said that was enough, he was hungry.

Louise and I left the sled in her backyard and went into the house for cocoa and Christmas cookies. Mrs. Martin had her best dress on and she looked rosy and plump and happy. Mr. Martin was fixing Jeff's remote-controlled car. Jeff is Louise's thirteen-year-old brother. We hardly ever see him because he's mostly off with his friends.

The snow stayed for a week, which it seldom does in western Washington. Mother made me work on reading in the mornings, but Louise and I went sledding every afternoon. We saw Jimmy and Leon on the hill by my house. Jimmy rode down with me a few times and Louise asked Leon if she could ride with him. She doesn't like to be with Jimmy because she says he's too short. That doesn't bother me. He'll go down from the top of the hill; Leon always wants to start in the middle.

The day it rained was the day vacation ended. Back to Mrs. Lobb and semester tests. The tests came the last week of January, and I might as well have played in the snow the whole holiday for all the good my reading practice did me.

Color the School Black

I didn't lift a book until report cards came back from the computer. Mother appealed to Dad to make me, but he wouldn't. He said we all might be on the wrong track.

There must have been some faint hope left in my heart. It beat wildly from eleven o'clock to three-twenty on the day the cards were delivered. At noon I poked at the tuna fish and noodles until Jimmy turned around to ask if he could please have my bun and cake before I messed up the whole lunch. I passed him my tray.

Recess, reading, health, and music dragged by until at last the day was over. Mrs. Lobb stood in front of the class with our cards. She called up each student in alphabetical order. Brown, Cannard, Hanson, Hinkler, Ingram . . . Jimmy grinned at me before he sat back down. He must have done all right. Jackson, Jenson, Keller, Mathews, *Nichols*. I stumbled getting out of my desk. When I reached for my card, it seemed almost as if Mrs. Lobb wanted to hold onto it a while. I kept my hand out until she gave it to me.

I didn't look at my report until I was back in my seat. Reading—F, Spelling—F, Social Studies—F, Arithmetic—B, Health—D, P.E.—S, Art—S, Music—S, Citizenship—U. Comments: *Helen is working below the sixth-grade level in the majority of her academic subjects. If she continues at her present rate of progress, she will not be promoted to junior high.*

I slapped the card face-down on my desk.

Jimmy turned around to see how I did. When he saw my face, he asked with a worried look, "You O.K.?"

I managed a nod.

The bell rang. I got stiffly to my feet, went to the closet for my jacket, and headed for the door without seeing anyone. As I left the room, I heard Mrs. Lobb call out, "Helen, may I talk to you a minute?"

I kept on walking. I didn't wait for Louise. I didn't wait for my mother's reaction. I handed her the card and went up to my bedroom.

Lying on my bed with my arm over my eyes, I half

listened to the phone conversation downstairs. "Mr. Douglas, please." I knew what she was going to say. She was going to say it was all Mrs. Lobb's fault and she wanted me out of that class.

She did. ". . . Obviously Mrs. Lobb has no understanding whatsoever of Helen's problems. . . . Yes, well, my husband and I are in entire agreement with you. If Helen doesn't do better under Mr. Marshall, we are going to seek other remedies. . . ."

Other remedies. The retard room, or a special school, or . . . what about me? I heaved off my bed and headed for the backyard where I couldn't hear her voice. I circled around the rotting corn husks, through the sagging raspberry lines, and over by the cherry tree. It would be awful to be left behind in that little school.

The door to the workshop was open. I stopped in the center of the floor to survey Dad's workbench. Black spray paint. SCHOOL MAKES ME PUKE. I snatched up the can.

I could smell dinner cooking when I returned. Mother was holding the lid to the frying pan with one hand while she forked over pieces of round steak with the other. "Where have you been?" she asked.

"I went for a walk."

"Without even telling me?"

"You were busy on the phone," I said. "When's dinner?"

"Just as soon as your dad gets home. Go wash your hands." She started to put the lid back on the pan. "Wait a minute. What's the black stuff on your finger?"

"Oh, that. I think it's paint. Dad's here." I escaped into the bathroom as Dad came in the front door.

The next morning, Louise and I had barely arrived at the sixth-grade unit when Stacy and Diane rushed up. "Hey, did you see the wall?" Diane asked.

"What wall?" Louise wanted to know.

"The back wall," Diane said. "Some kid spray-painted the school last night."

"Come on. We'll show you." Stacy led the way to the back of the school by the baseball field.

There it was in big black letters.

Louise put her hand up to her chin. "School makes me what?"

"Puke," Diane said. "Puke. So the kid couldn't spell."

Uh-oh. How do you spell "puke," I wondered.

At the entrance to our room, Leon came hopping up to me with his elbows flapping. "Puk puk a duck puk."

I pushed him out of the way. "What's with you?"

He hopped after me. "It's what school makes me do. Puk puk puk."

I didn't get it. "Jerk," I said, and took my seat.

Mrs. Lobb came into the room and looked over the class. "Helen," she nodded at me. "Please take your books in to Mr. Marshall's room."

"What?"

"You're assigned to Mr. Marshall's room this semester. Please clean out your desk."

Jimmy turned around. "Oh, no!"

I got the wastebasket to dump my old papers in.

"Do you have to?" Jimmy asked.

"I guess so." I stacked my books and pencils on top of my desk, put the wastebasket back, and took my jacket off the hook. "See you later," I told him.

As I walked up the aisle with my arms loaded, Jack said, "Lucky!"

Mrs. Lobb frowned.

I stopped at the door of Mr. Marshall's room and took in a big breath before I turned the doorknob. Louise's face lit up when she saw me.

"Is Helen coming in here?" Diane asked.

"That's right," Mr. Marshall said. "Helen, take any seat you would like."

"Sit with me." Diane shoved an empty desk up to hers. Desks were scattered any which way in this room. Not in straight rows like in Mrs. Lobb's.

I looked questioningly at Mr. Marshall.

"Anywhere you would like," he reassured me.

Louise was sitting with Stacy, so I dumped my stuff on the desk next to Diane.

"This is so neat," she said. "Now our room will win

all the games. Can we challenge Mrs. Lobb's room in
P.E. today?"

Mr. Marshall smiled. "Today we're beginning gym-
nastics. But we'll challenge them when baseball starts."

The door opened and Mr. Douglas walked in. There
was a deadly serious expression on his face which sent
fear through my insides.

"May I talk with the class for a few minutes?" he
asked Mr. Marshall.

"Certainly." Mr. Marshall moved over to his desk,
leaving the front of the room to Mr. Douglas.

"The first thing I would like this class to do is take
out pen and paper."

Jenny raised her hand.

Mr. Douglas nodded.

"Can we use pencil?" she asked.

"No. If you haven't a pen, borrow one." He waited
until everyone was ready. "Put your name in the upper
righthand corner. Next, I want you to print the following words: School makes me puke."

"You want us to write that?" a boy asked.

"Print it, please."

The boy shrugged and picked up his pen.

There was a catch to this, I knew. I printed carefully,
"School mak me puk," while thinking as fast as I could.
I had the word *school* right, I was sure. I practiced it

enough with Mother. But Louise couldn't read *puk* and Leon said *puck*. I sneaked a look at Diane's paper.

"Helen!" Mr. Douglas barked. "Keep your eyes on your own work."

My head snapped back like it was a rubber band.

"Now will you all pass your papers forward."

With my face burning, I quickly added an *es* to *mak* and an *e* at the end of *puk* before giving my paper to Diane to hand to the girl in front of us.

Mr. Douglas waited for our attention. "Most of you know that someone spray-painted our school last night. I suppose they may have thought it was funny. I don't think it was funny. I'm proud of our school and I hope you are, too. And I'm proud of the taxpayers, your parents, who support and pay for our fine school. I am sad that they have had an extra burden put on them. They are the ones who will have to shoulder the cost of restoring the wall."

His words made me cringe. I hadn't thought of the cost. How much would it be? Out of the corner of my eye I saw Mr. Marshall watching me, and I sat up straight to give Mr. Douglas my undivided attention until he left with our stack of papers.

I couldn't sleep much that night. I didn't think Mr. Douglas would know it was me by my printing. I'd used small letters instead of capitals as I had on the wall. But I was worried about the cost of repainting the school.

I wondered if I could do it? Or, if I told my dad, would he help me pay for it?

The next morning I was tired and barely listened to Louise talk on about how much I was going to like Mr. Marshall's room and how they were going to build rockets and go to the San Juan Islands the first of May. We were going to do those things in Mrs. Lobb's room, too, but I didn't say that to Louise.

As we walked up to the school, I caught sight of the janitor carrying a paint can and brush. I told Louise I'd see her later and I hurried after him.

"What are you going to do?" I asked, walking beside him.

"Oh, fix up that wall one of you kids messed up."

"Will it be very hard?"

"No, I'll just cover it up with a little paint."

"Where did you get the paint?"

"It was left over from painting the building last summer."

"How much do you think it will cost?"

"It'll take me about a half a can to patch it up. Say six dollars." He looked at me with raised eyebrows. "Why are you so interested?"

"I just wondered," I said, and faded back toward the front of the school.

During recess I took a good look at the wall. You couldn't even tell there'd been letters on it.

The Retard Room

Mr. Marshall stands in front of the room for silence like Mrs. Lobb. Only he doesn't make you feel guilty if you're trapped talking. He just waits patiently while the kids go "Shh, shh, shh," until the room is quiet.

It isn't a crime to ask someone for a pencil, but you can't act outright rowdy. When Diane threw a pen across the room to Jenny, Mr. Marshall said, "Diane, put your name on the board."

Diane got up immediately and wrote her name. Back in her seat, she took out a piece of paper and began writing over and over, "I will not throw things in the room."

"Why are you doing that?" I asked her.

"It's my punishment. You get to choose your own."

"Like what?"

"Like stay in at recess or after school, or clean up the room, or write an essay. Whatever you want." After she finished writing her sentence one hundred times, she handed the paper to Mr. Marshall and erased her name.

Even though we did fun things in the room like listening to a recording of wacko TV commercials and videotaping our own, a lot of the work was regular. That was the part that worried me.

In P.E. I did really well. When Mr. Marshall asked who could climb to the top of the rope, I went right up to the wooden circle on the gym ceiling. Because I could swing my legs over both parallel bars without touching, Mr. Marshall made me a spotter for the other kids.

Reading was different, though. I was just as dumb as I always was. I grew hot with embarrassment every time I had to hand in a written exercise. About the second week in his class, Mr. Marshall asked if I'd stay behind to talk with him while the other kids went out to recess. I knew what was coming.

"Helen," he said when the room was empty, "why don't you pull up a chair."

I pushed one close to his desk. He took the reading text from the shelf behind him, opened the book, and turned it toward me. "Usually I let students practice before they read aloud, but I'm going to ask you to read to me cold. Will you do that?"

"I'm dumb in reading."

"I suspected it was hard for you, all right. Do it for me anyway, O.K.?" He pointed to the top of the page. "Start here."

He let me stumble over every other word until I got to the end of the paragraph.

"That's about enough." He closed the book. "Reading *is* hard for you, isn't it."

"Yes, I'm dumb."

"You don't seem very dumb to me in gym."

"That's different," I told him.

"Or in math. I think you and Elsie are probably the smartest in the room in math." He folded his arms on his desk and leaned forward. "I don't understand why you turn letters around, but don't turn numbers around."

Mr. Marshall has gray eyes with curly black eyelashes. He looked at me with such interest, I relaxed. "I used to mix up numbers when I was in second grade. Sometimes I'd say twenty-one for twelve. My teacher told me to check the numbers real close so I wouldn't make a mistake. I still look real close at my answers. I don't mix figures up when I do them in my head."

"I've got a suggestion. Why don't we get help for you in reading. There's a teacher in this school who's trained to help students with problems like yours."

My insides sank. The same old thing. "You don't want me in your room."

He tipped up my chin with his big hand. "I like having you in my room. But I don't know how to teach students with special reading problems. Richard goes out for speech lessons. Couldn't you go out for reading lessons?"

"What about spelling and social studies?"

"O.K., you go out to the other room for spelling and social studies and reading and you stay here for everything else. I don't want to lose a good pitcher."

I tried to smile. "I have to go to the room for the dumb kids?"

"You don't have to. In fact, you can't unless you take some tests. I just think you need special help."

"My mother helps me every day at home."

"Are you getting any better?"

"Not much." He was cornering me and I knew it.

"I don't think you'd get any better with me, either. That's why I want you to go to a special teacher. How about going to visit the room with me today when the class is in music?"

I gave up. "I guess it can only kill me," I said.

Mr. Marshall looked startled. "I don't think it's going to be that bad, Helen."

It turned out he was right. The special room wasn't

bad at all. It wasn't as sloppy and warm as Mr. Marshall's room, but it wasn't clammy like Mrs. Lobb's, either. What interested me most were the three computers by the back wall.

There were two teachers and not many kids, maybe fourteen. One of the teachers seated Mr. Marshall and me near the computers. Just where I wanted to be! I watched a boy working one for a while. I think he was writing an essay.

He raised his hand and a teacher came up. "You're full steam ahead today, William," she said.

He scrolled his essay back to the beginning before he read it aloud to her. She stopped him a few times to have him look up the spelling in a dictionary. She stopped him again on the work *hike*. "William, remember to pay close attention to the endings of your words. A final *e* can make a vowel sound like its name. What you have would sound like *hick*. How do you make it *hike?*"

The boy pushed the insert button and added an *e*.

"And *mate?*" the teacher prompted.

And *puke*, I said to myself.

When the teacher left, I checked out the rest of the room. I didn't get a poster of a smiling man above the blackboard. He had a *d* for his left ear and a *b* for his right ear. Above his head was printed: Mr. *d----b----*.

The boy on the computer was busy so I leaned over to the boy in front of me. "What's that?"

The kid's eyes shifted across the blackboard where I pointed. "What?"

The picture of the man with letters in his ears. What's that for?"

"Oh, Mr. *db*. So we remember which way *d* faces and which way *b* faces."

"What if you forget and call him Mr. *bd?*"

"Then you're dead." The kid went back to work on his ditto sheet.

I figured you'd have to fill in the spaces between the letters to remember. I tried out *don't bawl*. I wouldn't mix that up with *bawl don't*. Or *dumb brain*. I could remember *dumb brain*.

There weren't many girls in the room, I noticed. One of them raised her hand and a teacher came up to correct her work. "That's great," the teacher said, "except for this one. Let me show you how the letter goes." The teacher held the student's hand and drew the letter in the air.

I wouldn't have to have *that* much help.

Walking back to our classroom, Mr. Marshall asked me how I felt about the visit.

"It was all right," I said cautiously. "But the ditto sheets looked like they were for little kids."

"Well, Helen, I think you have to start from where you are. You can't learn to throw a curve before you can get the ball over the plate."

That was true.

After school Mr. Marshall stopped me as Louise and I were leaving the class. "Have you thought any more about getting reading help?"

Mr. Marshall is real tall. He had his hand on my shoulder and I looked way up at him. "I don't think my mother would like it."

"How about letting me call your dad?"

"I guess that's O.K.," I said.

When we were out of his hearing, Louise asked me what that had been all about.

"Mr. Marshall took me to visit the special room," I told her.

Louise stopped in the middle of the walkway. "You mean you're going in with the retards? You don't have to, do you?"

"Not if I don't want to."

We were sort of quiet the rest of the way home. Mostly I was worrying about my mother, but for once she didn't pay any attention to me. She was rushing around the house moaning about her dirty hair while she flung clothes into a suitcase and called for plane reservations. Then she called Mrs. Martin to ask if I could stay with her after school the next week. I would

114

have liked to stay with Diane for a change, only this was obviously no time to argue. Uncle Leo had phoned that Grandma was worse, so Mother was flying to Denver to see her.

Dad and I drove her to the Sea-Tac airport. Riding back, I asked him if there was any job I could do the next morning, which was Saturday. For money, I added.

"A little short, huh? Well, I need to clean out my workshop. How about helping me with that?"

"How much do you pay?"

"Hmmm." He tapped the steering wheel with his fingers. "How about two dollars an hour? If you work hard."

"I'll work hard," I assured him. I knew the job would last three hours. He's real messy and hardly throws anything away.

After breakfast Dad got out a garbage sack and I got out the broom, rags, and dustpan and we went out to his shop. I hadn't been there since I took the paint. The place gave me a funny feeling.

He started the job by oiling his tools. I started out by dumping the empty cans and stiff brushes. He sat on a stool while I worked around him. "What are you going to spend the money on?" he asked me.

"I'm going to pay someone back."

"You owe somebody money?"

"Ya, well, sort of."

"Sort of?"

My dad can have a quick temper and I didn't want to set him off. "I'll tell you if you promise not to yell at me," I said.

"I promise."

"I did something bad."

"What did you do?"

"You promise you won't yell at me?" I was dropping three crooked nails, one at a time, into the garbage sack.

"I promise."

"I spray-painted the school."

The garden clippers he was oiling clunked down to the workbench. "You *what!*"

"You promised."

He picked up the clippers. "A . . . what did you write?"

" 'School makes me puke.' "

I thought I saw a smile quiver around his mouth.

"You're not mad?"

His face changed, drooping into sad lines. "Frankly, Helen, I don't see how you've stood it all these years."

It isn't easy not to cry when someone feels sorry for you. I turned my back on him quickly and went over by the door to get the broom. I kept my eyes on my sweeping as I said, "Maybe things are going to change. Can I tell you something else?"

"Sure."

"Mr. Marshall took me to visit another room. He thinks I should have a special teacher."

"That's what he said when he called me yesterday. What do you think?"

"Well." I swept a pile of dirt into a smaller and smaller circle. When I saw what I was doing, I went for the dustpan. "Well, it was funny. The kids in that class had exactly the same troubles I have. I never thought regular kids did. But Mother will hate it."

"She'll get used to it. Your mother worries too much about what people think. Most of the time people aren't even paying attention to what she thinks they are."

I wasn't sure about that.

Dad wiped his hands on a paper towel. "Why don't you take the weekend to decide. If you want to try working with the reading specialist, I'll go to school with you Monday morning to sign the permission for the tests."

"Mother said she'd never sign."

"Well, I will." He put his arm around me. "Come on. Let's eat lunch."

By the afternoon I had earned my six dollars for the paint and was sitting on my front steps worrying. It was going to be embarrassing to hand the money over to Mr. Douglas. But he wouldn't need all those people over for a discipline conference if I was going into the special room anyway.

After I finished worrying about Mr. Douglas, I worried about Mother and whether Grandma would die and whether all the kids would call me a retard. It started to rain. I was just about ready to go back in the house when Jimmy rode up on his bike. I invited him in.

"How do you like Marshall's room?" he asked when we were in the kitchen drinking Cokes.

"Beats Lobb's." I fiddled with the tab on the top of the can until I got up the nerve to tell him I couldn't decide whether to go into the special room or not.

"You better do something," he said. "You read just as bad now as you did in the fifth grade."

He was right, of course.

Mother's Girl

Mr. Douglas took Dad into his private office, leaving me outside on one of the chairs along the wall. The kids who came in with messages gave me knowing smiles. The secretary was there so I couldn't explain that I wasn't in trouble this time. At least I didn't think so. The six dollars was getting damp from being clutched so tightly in my hand.

Mr. Douglas and Dad came out the door. "Helen, I think you've made a responsible decision for yourself." Mr. Douglas beamed at me.

I stood up. "Yes, well, I have something to give you."

He took the money I held out to him. "What's this for?"

"It's for the paint used to cover up the printing on the wall." I inhaled a big breath. "That's how much the janitor said it cost."

Mr. Douglas didn't seem to know what to do. At first, the "Get-into-my-office-right-now" look came over his face, then he glanced at Dad, then back at me. "I hope you earned the money yourself."

"She did," my dad said. "And it was her idea."

"Good, maybe this is the end of 'Bad Helen.' " He looked expectantly at me.

I wasn't ready to go that far.

Dad held out his hand and Mr. Douglas took it. "It will take a while to get through all the paper work," he said to my dad. "And sometimes it's a month before the psychologist has an opening. We can't do anything until we get her recommendation."

"That's fine. We aren't in a hurry, are we?" Dad put his arm around me and walked me to the outside door.

It all happened faster than I was ready for. I was in music when the call came on the intercom for me to go to the office. The psychologist was waiting there. She had long red hair that hung down the back of her sweater. She gave me a big smile. "The student I was going to see today is absent, so I thought maybe you and I could get together, O.K.?"

I've noticed psychologists always act real friendly.

Even if you know this, they manage to get you talking anyway. We were barely in the library conference room before she had me telling her my whole life story, starting from when Mother kept me trapped in a playpen so I wouldn't total the house.

"Maybe you can remember when you're a parent," she said, "that little children need to crawl. It's part of their development." She had me kick a ball, toss a ball, catch a ball to see which hand and leg I used, I guess. She said I was surprisingly well coordinated and got me talking about how much I liked baseball.

Next we did reading and then she opened up her test kit. It looked the same as the one the psychologist at the University of Washington had used. Same blocks, puzzles, and cards. As she spread her things out on the table across from me, she asked, "You've had this test before?"

I nodded.

"Then we'll just zip through it."

When we were finished, she gathered up the materials and put them back in the box. "You're a smart girl."

"Not in reading," I told her.

"How you read doesn't have anything to do with how smart you are."

"What does it have to do with then?" No matter what you say to psychologists, they don't get mad.

"In your case it has to do with deficits in perceptual

121

processing, visual tracking, and visual discrimination or, in everyday words, how you see and understand and remember letters, words, and symbols. There have been lots of famous people with perceptual learning problems. Nelson Rockefeller, Thomas Edison, and Albert Einstein."

"And the special class will cure me?"

She laughed. "No, I don't think it's a cure. You're going to have to pay attention and work hard in there."

I sighed. Same old thing.

"But you'll be able to make progress," she assured me.

I didn't get it. "Why's that?"

"Because the work will be suited to you. No more slaving after school, after dinner, and all day Saturday. This teacher wants to teach you herself and has you practice at home for only fifteen minutes."

"Will she tell my mother that?"

The psychologist laughed again. "She sure will, and so will I."

I got up to leave and then I remembered and sat back down. "But what about passing? When do I get to go to junior high?"

"Next fall with the other sixth-graders. There's a resource room in the junior high where you can do your English and social studies. You'll do fine in regular classes with the other subjects."

I was so relieved at having only fifteen minutes of homework that I made the mistake of telling Louise. We were out in the backyard feeding her rabbits after school. She put the sack of pellets on top of the pen and stared at me. "You aren't really going in with the retards, are you?"

"Yes, I am!" I snapped. "I'm retarded in reading, you know."

"Well, you don't have to get so mad."

"I think I'll take off, now." I handed her the carrots.

Louise looked nervously at her watch. "It isn't time for your dad to be home."

"That's O.K. I'll walk slow."

She followed me around the side of the house. "Helen, I'll be friends with you even if you go in that room."

"Don't put yourself out,"I told her and left her behind.

I knew I wasn't going to feel like staying at Louise's house the next day. Luckily, I didn't have to. Mother called to say Grandma was better and she was flying home.

"What are we going to tell Mother about my going in that room?" I asked Dad.

He patted my hair. "Don't worry about it. I'll take care of that."

I sat on the upstairs landing and listened to him talk to Mother after I was supposed to be in bed. Taking care of it wasn't as easy as he would have liked me to think. Mother's hurt voice traveled up the steps. "I can't believe you'd do this behind my back without even talking it over with me."

"I didn't do it behind your back," Dad tried to explain over and over. "It just came to a head while you were gone."

"You could have waited a week. I think I should be a part of this."

"You will be," he said. "The psychologist and special education teacher want to meet with both of us."

Mother didn't say anything to me about the new room before the meeting or after the meeting. She didn't greet me at the door to ask, "How was school today?" She didn't look at my new reading book. I read it to myself.

I had to work hard in special education, like the psychologist said. Each morning we started out with our individual packets. On my ditto sheets there were letter combinations like the *cl* in cloud and clay and close. In Beth's packet there were sandpaper letters to trace with her fingers. Beth stayed in the room all day, so I didn't have a chance to make friends with her.

William, the boy using the computer when Mr. Marshall and I visited, stayed only for the reading subjects like I did. He was my age, but he was in fifth grade because he'd been held back in kindergarten. He and I usually walked back and forth to the class together.

On the fourth day, William was telling me a joke as we went out the door. He was feeling good because when the head teacher, Mrs. Tuttle, wrote on the blackboard, "Stand up, hop on your left foot three times, and place a pencil behind your ear," William did it the quickest. I was half listening to his joke and half wishing I'd started in special ed sooner so I could read faster, when I saw Dawn coming down the hall holding a note in her hand.

There was no way I could escape, so I said, "Hi," and she said, "Hi." After we'd passed I turned around to see where she was delivering the message. She had turned around, too, and was staring at me. Oh, boy, Dawn would tell Sharon and Sharon would tell her mother and . . . I could barely laugh at William's punch line.

When I sat down in Mr. Marshall's room, Diane asked me where I went every morning. "To the special ed room," I said, "to get help in reading and spelling."

"Oh, I noticed you couldn't spell. Listen, can you come over to my house after school? We'll ask Jack and Jimmy and see if we can get a baseball game going." Diane obviously didn't consider my reading problem a big thing, but that didn't mean the other kids wouldn't.

I looked closely at my mother's face before I asked her if I could go over to Diane's.

"I guess you can," she said.

When I got home from the game, I found Mother in the kitchen stirring a custard on the stove. She was moving the spoon so slowly in the pan, I had the feeling she had nothing else to do.

"Will you listen to me read for fifteen minutes?" I asked her.

She didn't answer me right away. I waited.

"All right." She put the spoon in a dish and turned off the stove. "Get your book."

After I finished reading, she sat quietly, looking down at the table. "You know, Helen, I really thought I could teach you."

I made my voice sound cheerful. "Well, we tried hard, didn't we?"

Things felt a little better between us then. That ended after dinner when I showed Dad the catalog Mr. Marshall lent me and asked him if I could order the seven-fifty rocket.

"Are all the students paying that much money?" Mother interrupted us.

"No, but Mr. Marshall will let you get any rocket you want. You can only get the little ones in Mrs. Lobb's room and she orders those so her kids don't get to see a catalog. The rockets are for our unit on flight," I explained.

"Well, I don't think you need one for seven dollars and fifty cents."

126

"Or maybe she does," Dad said.

Mother shot him a resentful glance. "I guess I'm extraneous." She left the room and went upstairs.

"What's extraneous?" I asked Dad.

"She feels left out." He held my arm to keep me from going after her. "Let's leave her alone awhile. She'll adjust."

She didn't seem to be adjusting very well to me. Dad brought it up the next evening. "I know how you can be *un*extraneous," he said to her while she was serving our dessert.

She sat down and slowly put her fork in her piece of custard pie.

"How is that?" she asked him coldly.

"I'm over-loaded, the secretary's over-loaded, the extra consultants are over-loaded. Everybody wants help with their returns under this new tax law."

Mother nodded toward me. "What about Helen?"

"I can take care of myself. I'm almost twelve."

She acted like she didn't hear me. "I suppose I could call Mrs. Martin and pay her for two hours a day."

"No, Mother." I leaned across the table so she had to give me her attention. "No, I'm big enough. I'll phone you as soon as I get home from school and I'll ask you before I go over to someone's house."

She thought a minute. Dad didn't say anything. I didn't say anything more.

"Well, I guess we can try it."

"Good," Dad said and looked right at her. "I really need you."

Before she took her bite of pie, I saw a little smile.

Big Mouth

When our rockets were finished, some of the kids from
Mrs. Lobb's room came in to see them before school
started. Jimmy, Leon, Jack, and Marianne gathered
around Diane's and my desks. "This is neat," Jimmy
turned my rocket around in his hand. "We only get to
build weeny ones."

"Ya, like you," Leon said. "Let me see it a minute."

"No!" Jimmy pulled away from him. "I'm looking at
it."

"Good paint job," Jack told me.

I'd painted my rocket shiny black and pasted U.S.A.F.
decals on it.

Sharon and Dawn came in the door. Sharon's eyes widened when she saw me and she gave Dawn a questioning look as they approached my desk. My stomach sickened, feeling what was coming.

"Helen, I didn't know you were still in here." Sharon pushed herself in beside Leon. "I thought you were sent to special ed."

"Just in the mornings, for reading subjects."

Dawn leaned over Sharon's shoulder. "My sister saw a TV show about dyslexia and they gave the kids some pills and then they could read. Why don't you try that?"

"My mother said," Sharon interrupted loudly, "that it was a crime the school didn't transfer you to a remedial room years ago and your parents should sue the school."

I reached out and took my rocket back from Jimmy.

"Maybe you'd get a pile of money if you sued." Sharon was looking straight at me, waiting for an answer.

I kept my attention on my rocket, as I set the fins carefully on my desk top. "The school couldn't transfer me without my parent's permission and my mother wanted to help me herself."

"Oh, look," Marianne said, "Elsie has a big rocket, too. Let's go see it."

Sharon didn't budge. "My mother said if you were in a special education class maybe you wouldn't get into so much trouble."

"So what?" Jimmy turned on her fiercely. "Do you know what *my* mother said? She said your mother's got a big mouth, and so do you."

Sharon's jaw dropped down. Before she could get herself together, Dawn dragged her across the room by the end of her pink sweater.

Diane watched them examining Elsie's silver and blue rocket. "I can't stand Sharon Hinkler," she said.

"Is your room going to camp?" Marianne asked.

"Of course," Diane answered. "Isn't your room?"

Leon smiled at Jack.

"Blob's still deciding about me." Jack sighed. "You're lucky you haven't got her."

"She'd never let Hel go," Leon said.

After the bell rang, Diane turned to me. "How many earrings do you have, anyway?"

"Three pairs. My Uncle Leo gave them to me for Christmas."

She eyed the green stones. "I like these best."

I knew Diane and Marianne tried to save me from being embarrassed, but it didn't help much. When Mr. Marshall had taken roll and read the bulletin, I got up slowly to start off for the special education room.

I met William as he was coming out of the fifth grade unit. "What's the matter with you?" he wanted to know.

"Oh, a girl was giving me some junk about being a retard."

William walked along beside me awhile before he said quietly, "In the fourth grade, everytime I left for reading or came back, one kid would say, 'There goes William off to his peanut college. Here comes William back from his peanut college.'

"I wanted to quit and my dad said I could, but he also said to remember that after I got out of school I didn't have to read books anymore, but, if I wanted to keep a job, I'd better be able to read directions and messages and receipts and sales slips." William pulled open the door of the special ed room for us and we went in and took our seats. A student monitor was passing out the reading folders.

"I'll take Raymond, Ken, and William at the back table first," Mrs. Tuttle said. "The rest of you will be able to find where you left off yesterday. Mrs. Julian will check your activities as you finish them."

I opened my folder. The next activity I had to do was write my vocabulary list "neatly two times." While I was working, I could hear Mrs. Tuttle pronounce each word she wrote on the blackboard for William's group. In this room hard words were explained *before* you read aloud.

William read his page easily until he came to "*live* in a boathouse."

"Sometimes we pronounce that word like '*live*

panther.' '" Mrs. Tuttle said. "But that doesn't make sense this time, does it."

"Live!" William corrected himself. " 'Live in a boat-house.' "

"Good! You're doing great. Go on."

"Helen, are you ready for me to check you?" Mrs. Julian was by my side.

"Oh, oh, yes." I came to and pushed my ditto sheet toward her.

She placed her initials by the side of my work. "And what do you do next?"

I read #2 under Selected Activities. " 'Write your word list in alphabetical order.' "

"Perfect. Now which one comes first?"

I looked carefully down the list. There were no words starting with the letter A. "*Bushes,*" I told Mrs. Julian.

"Good girl." She moved across the room to Beth, who had her hand raised.

When the reading groups were finished and the folders were collected, Mrs. Tuttle told us that today we were going to have psychology instead of social studies. I thought, Oh, no, not those blocks again.

"What I want you to do first is to take out a piece of paper and write down the traits of people you admire," Mrs. Tuttle explained. "You can choose your friends, rock stars, relatives, characters in stories—choose anyone you admire, alive or dead, and list the things in them you admire most. Got it?"

We nodded and took out our pencils and paper while she wrote our names across the blackboard. I thought first of Jimmy. I admire him because he's daring. I admire Mary Lou Retton because she's good in sports. Uncle Leo never says anything bad about anybody. Neither does Marianne. Both work hard, keep at it.

Mrs. Tuttle called on William to read his list. He said he admired his dad because his dad's kind and thoughtful. Mrs. Tuttle wrote "kind and thoughtful" under William's name.

"And I admire Eddie Murphy because he's funny." She added "sense of humor."

When Mrs. Tuttle got around to me, I said, "Daring, doesn't gossip, good in sports, and keeps at it."

Mrs. Tuttle wrote the list under my name on the board, only she changed "good in sports" to "athletic" and "keeps at it" to "persistent." After everyone had a turn, she asked us if we noticed anything about the words under each student's name. I stared at the board. I couldn't see anything wrong.

"I got it! I got it!" Beth yelled.

"What have you got?" Mrs. Tuttle asked.

"William is funny sometimes, and he's thoughtful and kind."

Mrs. Tuttle gave Beth a huge smile. "Wonderful.

And does that go for everyone's list? Are the traits you admire in other people the ones you have yourselves?"

I must have looked uncertain, because Mrs. Tuttle said to me, "Why did you write down 'daring'?"

"Because my friend Jimmy will start his sled at the top of a steep hill instead of halfway down."

"Do you start at the top?" she asked.

"Of course." I answered before I thought, and all the kids laughed.

By afternoon, when Mr. Marshall's class marched into music, I was feeling better. Miss Sleek noticed my earrings, too. "Oh, apple-green jade," she exclaimed when Diane and I filed past her. "That's my favorite gem."

Miss Sleek pulled me toward the podium while the rest of the kids were finding their seats. "Can I see?"

I took out one of the earrings and dropped it in her hand.

"Where did you get them?"

"In a jewelry store in the University District. The saleslady said jade would help my eyes. Do you believe that?"

"Maybe it's just another trip, but I think if you believe it, it will help." She gave me back the earring. "I better get the camp songs started."

That night I lay awake in bed a long time. I thought over Mr. Marshall's class, and Mrs. Tuttle's class, and

Mrs. Lobb's class, and reading aloud in a regular room, and getting teased about the special ed room, and what William's father had said. I didn't think Sharon would go at me again, especially in front of other kids, but there'd be looks and whispers.

The special ed room wasn't as fun as Mr. Marshall's room. Mostly it was hard work, but I *was* persistent and I could do it. And besides, if I stayed in there I didn't have to study after school and I got to go to junior high without summer school again.

But what would kids say when I went into a resource room in junior high for English and social studies like the psychologist said. But if I didn't go there, could I pass? And I knew you had to pass to play sports in junior high. If I were in a regular English class in junior high, the kids would know fast enough that I was dumb in reading anyway.

Face it, Helen, I told myself, you're dumb in reading. You've got a reading problem. You might as well stay in special ed and get help. And besides, I wasn't the only one with problems. Sharon had a personality problem and didn't even know it.

I turned over in bed, poked a dent in my pillow for my head, and went to sleep.

The Next-to-the-Last Firecracker

The next day, our class shot off the rockets in the base-ball field. Elsie's and mine went the highest. Everything we did after that had to do with "outdoor education," at least in Mr. Marshall's room.

It cost fifty dollars to go to camp, for the ferry ride, the food, and all. Some kids had trouble paying that much so the sixth-grade rooms collected aluminum cans and old newspapers. The day we took the newspapers out to the big trailer truck everything got into a mess.

Warren, Sharon, Leon, and Marianne were supposed to undo the string and put the bundles of newspapers in a neat stack so Jack, Jenny, Diane and I could carry them to the trailer. The rest of the kids were working inside the trailer or were emptying newspapers out of the parents' cars as they drove up.

The relay would have gone smoothly except Leon left for the bathroom and Warren just flung the papers toward a pile after he cut the string, while Sharon stood with both hands on her hips screaming at Warren for not doing it right, and Marianne dived around trying to catch the flying papers.

By the time Mrs. Lobb and Mr. Marshall got over to see what was holding up the line, the wind had blown newspapers all over the parking space. The sixth-graders never got a recess that morning. It took us until lunch to pick up all the mess. I was glad no one in our room had been stacking. Poor Marianne had to stand there while Mrs. Lobb lectured the goof-offs.

Mother said as long as I was going to camp for a week, she might as well work until my summer vacation. This pleased Dad and, to celebrate, he planned a dinner in Seattle. Unfortunately for Mother, he included the Lindstroms. Mother fussed with her hair and stewed over her dress until I told her, "All it can do is kill you."

She looked away from the bathroom mirror to where I was teetering on the edge of the tub. "That's a big help," she said, totally annoyed.

I shrugged. "Uncle Leo thought it was."

Mother went back to fussing with her hair. "Leo isn't the brainiest thing around."

I don't know about that. He gave me the nerve to visit the special ed room.

The week before camp, Mrs. Tuttle let me borrow a cardboard copy of a keyboard to practice on, so I could use the computer when I returned. Mother helped me with that after work. She also helped me pack the night before I left.

I put the items in my suitcase while Mother checked them off the "Personal Inventory Sheet for Outdoor School." She kept a sharp eye out to see that I packed only the acceptable extras like the camera she gave me and not any "Do Not Bring" extras like candy, gum, matches, or money.

"Raincoat and hat." She was reading the last of the list.

I went to get them.

"And boots. Take your boots if you're going fishing."

I was in the closet so she couldn't see my smile. I hadn't been feeling bad lately, so I hadn't been thinking of bad things to do. But, since Mother was watching for trouble . . . I carefully held the rubber boots upright as I took them out of the closet.

"That's everything," she said. "Let's lock it up. And you better go to bed because we have to be at the school at seven-thirty."

It was in the morning that I stopped by the cupboard to get the matches. I carefully tucked them down the front of my side-splitter T-shirt before I went into the dining room to drink my orange juice.

On the way up to camp we had a school bus all to ourselves. The high school counselors rode with us. The mothers and teachers rode in cars behind the bus. It was an hour's trip to Anacortes and by the time we got to the ferry dock, kids were leaning out the bus windows yelling, "Let us out of this jail!"

I took a picture of the big white ferry, Kaleetan, as it came into the landing, and a picture of a seagull perched on a pier. On the ferry, Diane, Stacy, Louise, and I sat together at a table on the upper deck to eat our sack lunches. When we stopped at Shaw Island, Jimmy came running up to us. "Hey, there's nuns on the dock pulling on the ropes."

We rushed out to the railing with my camera. Louise said there was a tiny chapel by the landing and the Franciscan nuns had the job of tying up the ferries.

The San Juan Islands are supposed to be sunny because the Olympic Mountains shield them from the rain coming in from the Pacific Ocean. But this day the sky was gray, the water was gray, and the clouds hanging over the trees on the islands were gray. It took over an hour to get to Orcas Island and another half hour to ride to Moran State Park. We screamed in relief when we saw the arch at the entrance to the camp.

After we unloaded the bus, Mr. Marshall called us to a meeting on the benches circling the campfire pit. He explained the borders of the camp grounds and told us the boys' cabins were off limits to the girls and the girls' cabins were off limits to the boys. The park ranger gave a lecture about not touching the fawns we might see in the woods. He said it would kill them if we brought them to the campsite because we couldn't put them back in exactly the right spot and the mother deer wouldn't find her baby.

Mr. Marshall showed the boys where their cabins were and Mrs. Lobb showed the girls. In ours we had eight bunk beds with plastic-covered mattresses. The floor was concrete and there were little screened windows looking out on the madrona and fir trees.

By the time we were unpacked, the sun had come out, so we put on our bathing suits. We saw Sharon leave the cabin beside ours as we went down the path. She had a green swimming mask on her forehead, green flippers in her hand, and a towel covering the lower half of her body. "What's the towel for?" Diane said. "Sharon's straight like a toothpick."

Mrs. Lobb looked even weirder. Her bathing suit ended in a skirt and under it blue veins traveled around her milkwhite legs like rivers on a map. She reminded us to wait for our high school counselors before going down to the beach. We did.

All the high school counselors had been to camp before, except one teenage boy. They initiated him at the campfire that night. When we had finished the songs, the stories, and the awards (Jenny got the Lung Award for her screams when I took a picture of her in the shower), one of the counselors called up the new boy.

He stood the boy beside the campfire, put a funnel into the top of the boy's pants, tipped his head back, and placed a dime on his forehead. The new counselor was to jerk his head up so the dime dropped in the funnel. He did it two times.

The third time, the old counselor told the boy to keep his head back with the dime on his forehead until we counted to ten. As we chanted, "One, two, three, four . . . " someone handed the old counselor a coffee tin of water which he poured down the funnel and into the boy's pants. We all whooped and hollered and Jimmy fell off the end of a bench laughing.

When campfire was over, Diane and I walked through the trees back to our cabins. Keeping my voice low so the girls behind us couldn't hear, I told her about the firecrackers in my boot.

"Wicked!" Diane said. "Let's throw the M70 into Jack's cabin tonight."

We waited until everyone was in bed and the two girl counselors had returned to the campfire before we crept out of our bunks. Unfortunately, the plastic-covered mattresses crackled with every move. "Where are you guys going?" Louise whispered.

"Out for a minute," Diane whispered back.

We didn't dare switch on our flashlights and we bumped into bushes and trees, giggling our way up the path to the boys' cabins.

Diane and I stopped at the sound of footsteps ahead. A flashlight blinded my eyes.

"What have you got there, Helen?"

"Where?"

"In your hand." Mr. Marshall's voice chilled me.

I held out my left hand.

He took the matches. "And the other hand," he said in that cold, quiet voice.

I gave him the firecracker.

"Now turn yourselves around and go back to your cabin and don't come out until morning. I'll see you both in the dining hall after breakfast."

We turned ourselves around and headed back down the hill with our flashlights on. "I wonder if he'll send us home," Diane said.

"Me, not you," I told her.

"My mother will kill me."

"*Your* mother will!" I had a feeling mine wouldn't be blaming the teacher this time.

I couldn't sleep. Worse than the thought of going home was knowing Mr. Marshall didn't like me anymore. I wiggled and turned for hours until Elsie yelled, "Shut up!" After that I held myself rigid in my sleeping bag, waiting for the sun to sift through the little cabin windows.

Diane and I stayed at our table when the other kids left the dining room. Mrs. Lobb gave us a questioning look. I hated Mrs. Lobb's knowing I'd broken the rules.

Mr. Marshall took Diane outside first. When they returned, Diane headed straight for the kitchen. I figured she'd gotten off by helping the cooks.

Mr. Marshall led me down to the campfire circle and sat me on a bench next to him. "Didn't you like camp, Helen?"

"Yes." My voice came out squeaky so I cleared my throat.

"Don't you like it in my room?"

"Yes."

His face was solemn as he looked down at me. "I don't understand then. I don't understand why you did this."

The tight band around my chest didn't mean I was going to cry. I never cry.

"Why, Helen?"

I swallowed.

"Why?"

"I guess it's just h-habit." And then it happened. A jagged breath caught at my throat. I put my hand quickly over my mouth, but I couldn't stop the sobs and I couldn't stop the tears. I bowed my head between my shaking shoulders and cried and cried and cried.

I heard Jimmy's worried voice near us. "What's the matter with Helen?"

"She'll be all right. You get ready for the hike." Mr. Marshall put a handkerchief into my hand and I covered my eyes with it.

"Wh-what are you going to do with me?"

"What do you think should happen to you?" he asked.

"I have to go home."

"Is that what you think you should do?"

"I guess so." Tears started down my face again. "I never cry."

"Crying doesn't hurt you."

I tried to focus on his face. "What I hate most is your not wanting me anymore."

"Helen, you broke the camp rules and I think you should make amends. But that doesn't mean I don't want you anymore." He took the soaked hanky and wiped my cheeks. "I'm going to coach a girls' baseball team this summer and I thought you might want to be my pitcher."

"Really?" I blinked the rest of my tears away. I *could* join a team this year, since I didn't have to go to summer school.

"Really. Now, what are you going to do about bringing a firecracker and matches to camp?"

"Maybe I could work in the kitchen every day and not go on the hike to Mount Constitution or swimming or fishing."

Mr. Marshall nodded. "I think it's fair that you miss the hike today and the swimming this afternoon."

"That's all?"

He got up. "That's enough. You go on up and ask the cooks what you can do. And don't leave the kitchen while we're gone without asking their permission."

"Oh, I won't," I told him and dashed up to join Diane.

We were both angels for the rest of the week. In fact, I was perfect for the rest of the semester in Mr. Marshall's class. I didn't even shoot off my third firecracker on the last day of sixth grade.

I saved it for junior high.

Barthe DeClements says, "Sometime during each of my grade-school years, the teacher would take her pitch pipe from her desk and call up the students, one by one. After she blew 'do-re-mi' on her pipe, the student was expected to sing 'do.' I stood beside each teacher each year with a heated face, having no idea where 'do' was.

"Years later, working as a psychologist in the Seattle School district, I tested children who may have been able to sing on tune but wouldn't have been able to read the scales. One ten-year-old boy threw up each morning before going off to another day of failure in the public schools. I recommended that he be transferred to the special education class. When I asked his teacher how he was doing in his new assignment, she told me, 'We didn't transfer him. I couldn't place that nice little boy in that awful class!'

"With the memory of the boy in my heart, and the memory of the approaching moment of the pitch pipe, I wrote the story of 'Bad Helen.' "

Ms. DeClements lives in a log house, built by the youngest of her four children, on the Pilchuck River near Snohomish, Washington.